TEXAS HORSETRADING CO.
HANGTREE PASS

Also by Gene Shelton
in Large Print:

Tascosa Gun
Texas Horsetrading Co.

TEXAS HORSETRADING CO.

HANGTREE PASS

GENE SHELTON

G.K. Hall & Co. • Thorndike, Maine

Published in 1998 by arrangement with
The Berkley Publishing Group, a member of Penguin Putnam Inc.

G.K. Hall Large Print Western Series.

The text of this Large Print edition is unabridged.
Other aspects of the book may vary from the original edition.

Set in 16 pt. Plantin by Al Chase.

Printed in the United States on permanent paper.

Library of Congress Cataloging in Publication Data

Shelton, Gene.
    Hangtree Pass : Texas Horsetrading Co. / Gene Shelton.
      p.   cm.
    ISBN 0-7838-0136-X (lg. print : hc : alk. paper)
    1. Large type books.   I. Title.
   [PS3569.H39364H3   1998]
    813'.54—dc21   98-5788

TEXAS HORSETRADING CO.
HANGTREE PASS

ONE

Brubs McCallan landed facedown between two rows of turnip greens, scooped up a mouthful of dirt, and bounced on his belly into a squash mound.

He lay stunned for a moment, the wind knocked from his lungs by the fall. He heard the uneven hoofbeats as the big sorrel bucked back toward the remuda fifty yards away.

Brubs tried to sit up — and panicked. He couldn't move from the shoulders down. Then he realized his arms were pinned to his sides by what seemed to be a mile and a half of petticoats, his legs shackled by a twisted sheet. He finally managed to suck in a quick breath of air, spat out a glob of dirt, and let the panic fade. He heard rapid footsteps approach and tried to relax as a shadow fell across the squash plant leaves.

"Get me out of this, Dave," Brubs gasped. "I'm plumb tied up like a brandin' calf —" The plea ended in a startled squawk as something whapped into the back of his neck, driving his face deeper into the sharp, pointy leaves.

"You young whippersnapper!" The voice was female, but it boomed out like a bullwhacker's shout. A blow thumped into the back of Brubs's neck; an instant later another whopped against his left ear. "Tear up a poor old" — *whop* — "widow woman's garden" — *whop* — "mess up

7

her fresh laundry" — *whop*.

Brubs finally managed to lift his head far enough to glance over his shoulder, just in time to catch the full impact of the broom between the eyes. He tried to lift a hand to ward off the blow, but it was trapped tight against his side. Brubs heard a hoot of laughter from nearby between swats from the broom.

The beating abruptly stopped.

Brubs managed to roll onto his side and squint through the grit on his eyelids. Dave Willoughby had his arms wrapped around the waist of an aging woman, trying to pull her away from Brubs. Willoughby had his hands full. Dave stood six foot two and carried a hundred and seventy pounds of muscle on his lean frame. The woman was nearly as tall as Willoughby, and considerably heavier and wider. Willoughby ducked a backward poke of the broom handle.

"Take it easy, ma'am," he said with a wide grin, "there's no need to beat poor Brubs to death."

"Take your hands off me!"

"If you promise you won't hit my friend with that broom, I'll release you."

For a few seconds the old woman glared at Brubs, her broad face splotched red in anger, the long-handled broom poised for another swing. Then she sighed. "All right, young man," she said softly.

Willoughby turned her loose.

She spun on a heel and whacked Willoughby

alongside the head with the broom. "I didn't promise I wouldn't hit *you*," she snapped.

Willoughby squawked and backpedaled, his hands held out before him in supplication. The woman stalked him with the broom held at shoulder height as if it were a Comanche lance. "Ma'am, please," Willoughby said, "we mean you no harm. It was all an unfortunate mishap. My friend seems to be drawn to accidents like a moth to a flame."

"When you two get done waltzin' around," Brubs called, "how about givin' me a hand here? I ain't got nothin' against havin' petticoats wrapped all around me, but this ain't exactly the way I like 'em."

The woman turned away from Willoughby and glowered at Brubs. "You ought to be ashamed of yourself," she said. "You tore up half my garden and ruined my wash."

"Well, ma'am, I'm truly sorrowful," Brubs said earnestly, "but I honest to Pete didn't ask that fool sorrel horse to buck me off right here." The grit in his mouth and dirt on his tongue hobbled his words a bit. "Old Squirrel ain't usual one to pitch, and I reckon he wouldn't have if that damn rooster of yours hadn't run a-squawkin' and a-flappin' between his front feet."

The anger splotches slowly faded from the woman's face. Her shoulders slumped. Brubs was surprised to see tears pool in her eyelids. "That garden is all I have left since my poor Herman died," she said. "I was counting on it to see me through the winter. I just yesterday finished fertilizing it. It took me all day to spread that chicken manure."

Brubs spat frantically.

"And I spent all morning doing that wash. Now it's got to be done over again."

Dave Willoughby removed his hat. "Don't you worry, ma'am," he said. "We'll make it up to you. Now, if you don't mind, I would like to get the mummy here unwrapped and see if he's broken anything." Willoughby's cheek was still red from the whap of the broom, but he couldn't hide the amused twinkle in his eyes. Brubs McCallan was trying to scrape the dirt from his tongue against the petticoats wrapped tightly around his neck and shoulders.

The woman knelt by Brubs's side as Willoughby lifted him to a sitting position. "I'm sorry I beat you with the broom, young man," she said, "but I lost my temper. I spent so much work on that garden." She probed around, found the hem of a petticoat, and started unwrapping the garment from Brubs's shoulders.

"Chicken manure?" Brubs's upper lip wrinkled beneath his thick mustache. He spat again.

"It could be worse, Brubs," Willoughby said with a soft chuckle. "In some countries they use *human* waste to fertilize their gardens."

Brubs nailed Willoughby with a hard stare. "You are truly a comfort, Dave Willoughby."

Several minutes passed before the woman and Willoughby managed to unravel Brubs from the

10

tangled sheets and garments. Finally, he was able to stand. Everything still seemed to work. He tried not to think about the lingering taste in his mouth.

Willoughby suddenly reached out and placed a gentle arm around the old woman's shoulders. Tears flowed openly down her cheeks. "Ma'am, are you all right?"

She hiccuped a sob, then nodded. "I'm sorry to show such weakness. It's just that — well, last year I lose my Herman. This year I lose my Angela. And now this. . . ." Her voice trailed away.

"My sincere condolences over the loss of your husband, ma'am," Willoughby said softly. He gave her shoulders a gentle squeeze. "Was Angela your daughter, or perhaps a sister?"

"My mule." The woman hiccuped again. "Thieves took her, my Angela." She waved a hand toward a small barn beside the garden. The corrals stood empty except for a single jersey milk cow and a suckling calf in separate pens. A buggy with sun-faded black paint stood beside the barn.

Brubs snorted in disgust. "I never could abide no dishonest horse thief, 'specially one would steal a poor widder woman's only mule. It just ain't — ain't *ethical,* that's what."

"How will I work my garden? How will I get my buggy to town to sell my butter and eggs without my Angela?"

Willoughby dropped his arm from the widow's shoulder. "Ma'am, we just happen to have two

11

good mules in our remuda over there. It would be our pleasure to make you a gift of one of them — to replace your Angela."

"Dave, them's valuable mules!"

Willoughby cast a quick glance at Brubs, then turned to the woman. "If you will excuse us for a moment, ma'am, I would like to have a private conversation with my partner." He led Brubs out of the woman's range of hearing.

"Dave Willoughby," Brubs sputtered, "you are goin' to run us plumb into the poorhouse."

"Shut up a minute and listen to me, Brubs," Willoughby said. "It isn't as if we paid for both those mules. If you will recall, only one was in the group of ten animals we bought back in LaQuesta before we ran short of cash. And at any rate, we have no buyer for mules at the moment."

Brubs swiped a soiled palm across his stubbled cheek. "Reckon you're right there. It ain't like it would cost us nothin', you put it that way. That big mule was in the cavvy we stole from that rich grandee down to Sonora." He spat again and scrubbed a shirtsleeve across his mouth. "That old coot likely won't never miss the horses, let alone one mule." He shrugged. "Guess it wouldn't hurt none to do a poor widder a good turn."

The two trudged back to where the woman stood leaning on the broom. Brubs flashed a quick grin at her. "Ma'am, my partner and me want to give you one of our mules. Compliments of the Texas Horsetradin' Company. That's us."

The old woman's hiccuping sobs slowly faded. "That's kind of you," she said, wiping a knuckle across her damp cheek.

Willoughby reached into a shirt pocket and pulled out a coin. "Would ten dollars compensate you for the damage done to your garden, ma'am?"

"Dave Willoughby!" Brubs squawked. "You flat out lied to me! You told me we was broke!"

Willoughby sent one of his *shut-the-hell-up* looks at Brubs, then handed the coin to the woman. She fondled the gold piece for a moment, then nodded and dropped it into a pocket of her dress. "I am sure," Willoughby said sincerely, "that my friend would gladly redo the wash for you —"

"Dave," Brubs squalled in protest, "don't get so plumb carried away with this milk of human kindness stuff!"

"Except that," Willoughby said, ignoring Brubs's interruption, "we really must be on our way. We have a buyer waiting to purchase our horses, and it isn't good business to keep a customer waiting."

Brubs glanced toward the remuda. The animals had drifted off another thirty yards and now grazed leisurely at the rich green grass along the creek that ran toward Fredericksburg less than two miles away. Brubs's sorrel saddle horse grazed along with them as if nothing had happened. Brubs brushed at his clothes, stooped to pick up his battered hat, and ran a hand through his thick, unruly shock of sandy hair. "Mighty sorry about this, ma'am."

"Permit me to perform the formal introductions, madam," Willoughby said. "My somewhat grubby friend here is Brubs McCallan. My name is Dave Willoughby."

"I'm Helen Richter, widow of Herman Richter." The woman's tone softened a bit as her anguish faded. She lifted an eyebrow at Willoughby. "You speak oddly."

"He's a Yankee, ma'am, and a college boy," Brubs hastened to explain, "but don't hold that against him. He ain't really a bad fellow despite it. I been tryin' to make a Texan out of him ever since I got him out of that San Antonio jail, but so far it ain't took. He's makin' some progress though."

Helen Richter turned a cold look on Willoughby. "Jail, yet? I would expect that from your friend here, Mr. Willoughby, but you seem to be a decent, clean-cut young man."

"Mrs. Richter, Brubs has a way of getting things turned around somewhat on occasion. Quite a lot of the time, in fact," Willoughby said. "It really wasn't anything serious. A slight quarrel over a question of integrity that got a bit out of hand."

"We caught a cowboy cheatin' at poker and busted up a saloon," Brubs said. "Dave here likes to dress things up in fancy words sometimes. Like he said, it didn't amount to much." He

14

lifted an eyebrow at Willoughby. "We best get them horses movin' again, partner. It's a far piece from here to Drippin' Springs. You fetch that idiot horse of mine and that mule for Mrs. Richter, we'll be on our way."

Brubs glanced toward the small but well kept home and moaned aloud. The possibles sack he had been carrying when the sorrel fell apart lay between house and garden. The bottom of the bag was stained wet. Brubs hurried to the sack, opened the drawstring, and glanced inside, then mouthed a string of his most colorful oaths.

"Problem, Brubs?" Dave asked from the saddle on his black gelding, Brubs's sorrel and a leggy mule trailing behind on loose lead.

"This here is the saddest thing I ever seen," Brubs said with a slow shake of his head. "Busted the whiskey bottle. Only one I brought." He lifted the soaked cotton sack to his nose and sniffed longingly.

"Are the rest of the supplies ruined?"

Brubs cast a disgusted look at Willoughby. "No, dammit, but you sure got a funny idea of what supplies is important to a man. It's gonna get mighty thirsty 'tween here and Drippin' Springs." He lifted an eyebrow. "If you got any more money stashed back I don't know about, I'll go fetch another jug."

Willoughby shook his head. "That was the last of it, Brubs. Honestly. We are now broke. Officially, flatly without funds, even so much as a copper penny."

Brubs mounted, kneed Squirrel toward the re-muda, and said, "Dave, you got to quit holdin' out on me like that. Why, we could have had us a right fine good time with that ten dollars. I know two girls over to Fredericksburg —"

"Which is exactly why I held back the gold piece, friend," Willoughby interrupted. "I am well acquainted with the speed at which you separate us from our money where whiskey and women are concerned."

Brubs pouted in injured silence as the two rode toward the grazing horses. He glanced over his shoulder. The widow had already led the mule into the corral. "Seems to me," he finally said, "you was a might overgenerous with that old woman." He spat. "Ten dollars and a mule, too."

A slight smile touched Willoughby's face. "I was generous for two reasons. First, people in our business never know when we might need a friend. Horse thieves are not universally admired in Texas."

Brubs winced. "Now, Dave, you know it ain't like we was real horse thieves, the kind what steals from just anybody. We got higher standards than that. We buy some when we got money, and when we're broke we don't steal 'em from nobody who ain't stole 'em from somebody else. And the Texas Horsetradin' Company sure never stole none from a poor widder woman."

Willoughby cast a sideways glance at Brubs and ignored his partner's protest. "Secondly, I suppose you could say I've always had a soft spot for the poor and downtrodden."

Brubs snorted. "Then how come you signed on with the damn Yankee army? Seems to me wasn't nobody no poorer and downtrodden than us Southerners."

Willoughby's smile faded. "I did what I thought was right at the time, just as you did. Looking back, I suppose we were both wrong. We weren't alone."

Brubs said, "Hell, partner, that war's over. And that," he added, "is the only good thing about it. Let's get these broomtails movin'. Couple or three days we'll have us a bunch of silver janglin' in our pockets. Then we can get us a couple women and a jug and have some real fun."

Willoughby suddenly chuckled aloud.

"What's so funny?"

"What little episode back there," Willoughby said. "It was one of the most entertaining events — better even than the touring theater companies that appeared back home in Cincinnati."

"Glad you enjoyed it," Brubs groused. But a slight grin tugged at his lips. "I was sittin' a little too close to see it all myself."

"When that rooster ran between Squirrel's feet, it was like the curtain going up on a comedy in three acts," Willoughby said. "Act one was when he pitched into and then along the clothesline and wrapped you up like a butcher shop pork chop. Act two was when he bucked you off face-down amid the turnip greens. Act three was when that lady lit into your hide with that broom. It was quite a spectacular scene, in sum."

Brubs said, "Guess it was some wreck, at that. Just might be worth tellin' my grandkids about, I ever have any. That I know about." He reined Squirrel aside to push a stray gelding back into the horse herd.

"Do me one favor, Brubs," Willoughby called after him, "let me ride on the upwind side of you."

"How come?"

White teeth flashed in Willoughby's lean, clean-shaven face. "You smell a bit like the inside of a henhouse, my friend."

Brubs McCallan reined Squirrel to a stop and dismounted in front of Wes Langley's Slash L Ranch headquarters.

The cluster of native rock buildings and pole corrals nestled in a grove of cottonwoods, big oaks, and pecan trees against the side of a bluff overlooking the creek that flowed from the deep, clear pool that gave the place its name, Dripping Springs.

The place looked like something Langley would build if half the stories he had heard were true, Brubs thought. The buildings were rough and unpolished, but everything served a purpose. Wes Langley had put his ranch together one cow and one acre at a time, and the word around Texas was that Langley didn't bother to buy either the cows or the land. He just took what he wanted and backed it up with a Colt and a

Winchester. Rumors said a half dozen men who didn't want to give up their land to Langley got to keep part of it — a part six feet long, three feet wide, and as deep as Langley's crew felt like digging. Now Langley had control over twenty thousand acres of prime, well-watered grassland. He also had a dozen or so rough-edged hard cases to help him hold it.

A big, broad-shouldered man in the garb of a working cowboy lounged on the porch of the main house, a Winchester rifle crooked in his arm, a Colt Peacemaker holstered at his hip, and a suspicious look in his one remaining brown eye. The socket where the other eye should have been was a mass of ridged scar tissue striped by a jagged white line that ran from hatband to stubbled chin.

"Howdy," Brubs said, propping a boot against the lower porch stop. "The boss around?"

The brown eye narrowed. "Who's asking?"

"Brubs McCallan, Texas Horsetradin' Company. We brung the horses Mr. Langley sent word he needed. My partner's holdin' the cavvy a ways downstream."

The one-eyed man stared for several heartbeats at Brubs, then turned and tapped on the frame of the open door. "Jasper out here wants you, boss. Says he brought some horses."

Brubs heard a rumbling mutter from inside the house. Moments later Wes Langley stepped onto the porch. Langley didn't look like one of the richest men in Texas, Brubs thought. Langley wore regular working cowboy's range clothes and a battered, sweat-stained hat. He carried a Smith & Wesson New American .44 in a worn at his left hip. He stared at Brubs for several seconds, his pale blue eyes cold beneath bushy gray brows.

"You McCallan?" Langley's voice was a growling baritone, like a grizzly prodded from late-winter hibernation.

"Yes, sir."

"Got the horses?"

"Thirty head." Brubs waved a hand downstream. "My partner's holding 'em just round the bend of the crick."

Langley glanced at the one-eyed man. "Hake, roust a couple boys from the bunkhouse and fetch the horses. Put them in the big corral."

The man called Hake grunted, cast a quick and cold glance at Brubs, then strode with a noticeable limp around the corner of the house.

"That there," Brubs said, "is a man with a mad on if I ever seen one. His drawers always in a wad?"

"Hake's got his reasons," Langley said. He pulled a crook-stemmed pipe from a vest pocket. "Don't mess with him. Hake hasn't been right in the head since the Comanches worked him over thirty years ago. That's when he lost the eye and got the limp." Langley opened the drawstring of a soft leather pouch with his teeth and dribbled tobacco into the pipe bowl. "Hake's been even grumpier lately. His favorite nephew got killed down near Goliad a spell back. Fellow by name of Jake Clanton."

A chill scooted up Brub's back. He knew about Jake Clanton. He and Willoughby were the ones who had killed him. That Jake Clanton had deserved killing didn't change that uncomfortable little fact. Brubs swallowed hard. "Any idea who done it?"

Langley paused in the act of stuffing his pipe and studied Brubs for a moment, his eyes narrowed, then shook his head. "No witnesses. But Hake found a .44 Henry rimfire cartridge case beside what was left of Jake after the coyotes and buzzards got through with him. Not many people pack Henrys anymore."

Brubs swallowed again as Langley's gaze drifted to the .44 Henry repeater in Brubs's saddle scabbard. "Been thinkin' about gettin' me somethin' else, now you mention it," he said. "Lots better long guns on the market these days."

"That's a fact. I use one of those new Winchester 40-60's myself. Packs a nasty wallop. Makes a mighty ugly hole in a man." Langley tamped the tobacco with a thick finger and scratched a match against the porch support post. He shrugged, puffed the pipe into life, and shook out the match. "Bass Jernigan told my *segundo* you boys deal in good horses."

Brubs sighed in relief. He was getting a tad twitchy talking about .44 Henrys and dead Jake Clantons. "I was wonderin' where you heard about us. We sold Bass some mighty fine mounts a spell back. Bass is a good man. Knows his hossflesh."

Langley nodded, but the ice in his eyes didn't thaw. "Bass said you're okay. That's good enough for me until I see something to make me change my mind." He puffed the pipe into a full boil. "I work the same way Bass does. I look the horses over and quote a price. You take it or leave it. I don't haggle."

Brubs nodded. "Sounds fair by me."

The two waited in silence as Hake, two other Slash L hands, and Dave Willoughby penned the horses. Willoughby led the little gray mustang and big roan, now serving their turn as pack-horses.

Brubs studied Langley's face while the rancher counted the animals as they passed through the corral gate. A muscle in Langley's jaw twitched a couple of times. Langley raised an eyebrow and nodded toward the two packhorses.

Brubs shook his head. "The gray mustang and that roan ain't part of the sale bunch," he said. "Personal horses."

"I recognize the roan," Langley said. "Stump Hankins's horse. Choctaw."

"Yes, sir. Was Stump's, anyway. He give Choctaw to my partner." Brubs waved toward Willoughby. "This here's Dave Willoughby. We was mustangin' with Stump when he got killed."

Langley puffed hard on the pipe. His gaze drifted back to the horses in the corral.

"Them's some mighty fine mounts, Mr. Lang-ley," Brubs said. "Near ever one of 'em's broke to saddle. Why, most of 'em's good cow ponies too."

"I can see that, McCallan," Langley said. He plucked the pipe from his mouth and knocked the ashes from the bowl against a fence rail. "I can also see we've got a little problem here," he said.

Brubs frowned. "What might that be?"

Langley jabbed the pipe stem toward the remuda. "That brown over there. The one with the star and stocking feet."

"Best of the bunch," Brubs said eagerly. "Gentle, quick as a scorched cat, got a mess of cow sense, and a hell of a fine rope horse. Rode him myself a couple times."

"You don't have to tell me how good he is, McCallan." Langley's gaze turned colder. "I know that horse. He's mine. Some son of a bitch stole him a couple of months back."

Brubs's heart skidded as he heard the whisper of metal against leather and the distinct clicks of hammers drawn to full cock. He glanced around. Every one of the Slash L hands had a Winchester or revolver aimed at Brubs or Willoughby.

"Around these parts, McCallan," Langley said, his voice soft, "we hang horse thieves."

TWO

Dave Willoughby had always been impressed with the .45 Colt Peacemaker, but never so much as now. The bores of the handguns locked as big as badger holes. Especially when they were pointed at a man's gut.

"Now, gents," Wes Langley said, "you two shuck those gun belts — slow and easy."

Willoughby felt the quickening thump of his heart against his ribs and the cold, icy knot in his belly. He glanced at Brubs. The stocky Texan's face was pale, but his jaw was set, his eyes narrowed. He looked more mad than scared. Brubs lifted a hand. "Rein in a minute, Langley. We can talk this here little problem out."

"Save your wind, McCallan," Langley growled. "There isn't anything to talk about. You stole my horse." He turned to the one-eyed man. "Hake, get a couple of ropes over a limb of that big oak down at the spring. Same one we lynched the last two horse thieves on."

Hake's good eye glittered in anticipation. He limped to a pair of Slash L horses tied to the corral rails, slipped the tie thongs from saddle horns, and lifted two Manila hemp ropes. He formed a small loop in one of the ropes, glanced at Willoughby as if measuring his neck, and grunted in satisfaction. The look didn't help the twitches in Willoughby's belly.

24

"Mr. Langley," Brubs said earnestly, "I swear to God we didn't steal that there brown. We bought him, fair and square, down in Sonora. I'd sure hate to see somebody get hurt over such a little trifle."

"Trifle?" Langley snorted in disgust. "You think it's a trifle to steal a man's horse and then try to sell it back to him?"

Brubs sighed in resignation and glanced at Willoughby. "Dave, he ain't gonna listen to reason. Now, I know I promised you that you wouldn't have to kill nobody else unless you wanted to, but it's done out of my hands now. You take them three on the right."

"Brubs —" Willoughby could barely force a croak through the tightening in his throat. It felt like the noose was already shutting off his air. He glanced at the three men on his right. Two held cocked revolvers. The third had a Winchester in hand, the hammer eared back.

"I'll take Langley and this other jasper on the left." Brubs offhandedly nodded toward the gunmen. "Sorry, partner," he said to Willoughby, "I know it grates on you to have to shoot a man cold. Bothers me some, too, but I reckon ol' Wes here ain't givin' us no choice."

Amusement flickered in Wes Langley's pale blue eyes. "I'll grant you one thing, McCallan," he said, "you've got bigger *cojones* than a prime Mexican stud horse. Try to pull iron on five men who've already got you in their sights? Nobody's that fast."

"Brubs —"

25

"Dave is," Brubs said calmly, ignoring Willoughby's attempted interruption. "Now, I ain't in Dave's class with a handgun, but I reckon I'll hold up my end —"

"Dammit, McCallan," Willoughby all but yelled, "if you'll shut up a minute, we can settle this without anybody getting hurt!"

Langley's cold gaze shifted to Willoughby. "Well, I'll be damned," he said, "it talks."

"Mr. Langley, I have a bill of sale for that animal. As my partner said, we did not steal that star-faced brown. I have the bill of transfer in my saddlebag."

Langley said, "Let's have a look at it." His blue eyes narrowed. "And, son, you'd better not bring anything but paper out of that pouch or you'll be wearing more holes than a drifter's drawers."

Willoughby nodded. As he reached into the saddlebag he glanced across the horse's back. The one-eyed man had tossed two ropes over a stout oak tree limb a few yards away. The sight popped fresh drops of cold sweat across his forehead. Willoughby drew a deep breath, willed his fingers to stop trembling, and lifted a handful of folded papers from the pouch. He thumbed through the papers and handed one to Langley.

Langley's brow furrowed as he studied the bill of sale. "You know who signed this, Willoughby?"

"The man we bought the brown and nine other horses from. A Mexican horse trader."

26

Langley snorted in contempt and wadded the paper into a ball with a scarred fist. "Horse trader, my butt. That's Three-toe Ortega's mark on that paper. He's a bigger horse thief than you boys are. A damn sight smarter, too."

"What?" Brubs squawked indignantly. "You mean that pepper gut done went and sold us a stolen horse? Why, that's the meanest, rottenest, low-downest trick I ever heard of!" Brubs's ruddy face reddened in apparent anger. "When I get back to Sonora I'll skin that tamale-eatin' jackass alive and hang his hide on my barn door!"

A wry smile touched Langley's lips. "Looks like you boys have been took. So what do we do now? Old Hake's got his heart set on a good hanging. If we don't give him one, he's going to be some put out with us."

Brubs lifted himself to his full five feet seven, poised on the balls of his feet, his right hand near the Colt holstered at his hip. "Can't let you do that, Wes," he said. "Now, you can maybe hang me for bein' short. You can hang me for bein' ugly. You can hang Dave Willoughby for bein' a damn bluecoat Yankee. But, by God, you ain't gonna hang us for stealin' a horse we didn't swipe! Now, squat or get off the pot!"

Willoughby felt the tension mount until it carried the weight of a dead animal across his shoulders. All it would take to attract about a pound of lead, he knew, was one sudden move. He slowly raised a hand.

"Mr. Langley," Willoughby said, "Brubs and

27

I may not be the brightest people in the world, but do you really think we would be dumb enough to try to sell you a horse we had stolen from you in the first place?"

Langley's gaze flicked from Brubs to Willoughby and back again. The slight, amused smile was still on his lips. "Maybe, maybe not. Man who fools around with horses and cows can't be too bright."

A flicker of hope sputtered in Willoughby's chest. "Suppose we give you the brown, as a gesture of goodwill from the Texas Horsetrading Company? We will absorb the loss."

"Dammit, Dave," Brubs protested, "that brown cost us fifty whole dollars."

"The bill of sale said twenty," Langley said. His ice-blue eyes twinkled in growing amusement. "You just won't quit yanking on a man's blanket, will you, McCallan?" The hint of smile on his lips widened. "All right. You give me the brown back and I won't hang you or shoot you. Maybe I ought to, just on general principles and because I damn well know you didn't pay for all those horses. But I won't. Fair enough?"

Willoughby nodded and breathed a silent sigh of relief.

Brubs grunted an agreement. "I'll play. Wasn't too keen on us havin' to shoot you and your boys, anyhow. Bad for business, killin' customers."

Wes Langley turned to the grim-faced gunmen standing beside him. "Put up the hardware, boys.

Fun's over. One of you trot down and tell Hake the lynching's off."

Willoughby relaxed at the clicks of metal and whispers of steel against leather as the Slash L riders lowered hammers and reholstered weapons. One strode toward the one-eyed man waiting at the tree.

Langley turned back to Brubs. "Now that we have that settled," he said, "I'll make you an offer on the rest of the horses. I may lynch a man from time to time, but I don't go back on a deal."

"That's right neighborly of you, Wes," Brubs said.

"Damned if I know why," Langley said, "but I sort of like you boys, even if you are a couple of aces short of a full deck. Probably comes from getting bucked off headfirst in a rock pile one too many times." He chuckled aloud and rubbed a callused palm over the stubble on his chin. "Used to be a bit wild myself, back in my younger days. Let's take another look at these broomtails you boys brought in."

The one-eyed man limped up as Langley and Brubs leaned against the fence rail, studying the animals in the corral. Hake's good eye glittered in anger and his scarred face twisted in a deep scowl. Hake barely glanced at Willoughby, but stared long and hard at Brubs. The look in that eye would temper a horseshoe red-hot from the forge at twenty paces, Willoughby thought.

"That stocking-legged sorrel's wind-broke,"

Langley said, jabbing a finger toward a gelding at the edge of the remuda. "Can't use him for anything but wolf bait."

"He'd make a good buggy horse," Brubs said hopefully.

Langley glanced at Brubs. "Now just what in the blue-eyed hell do I need a buggy horse for? Long as I can fork a saddle I'm not even going to own a buggy. I'm not buying the sorrel." He turned back to the remuda. "I'm not taking the gray, either. He's outlawed. Got that look in his eyes like he's hunting a cowboy to kill, and more spur tracks than flies on his shoulder."

Brubs shrugged, then said, "Figured you'd spot them two right off. I do admire a man knows his hossflesh." Brubs stripped a thin splinter from a fence rail and tucked it in his mouth. "Okay. We'll trail them two back. Rest of 'em suit you?"

"Don't need a mule." Langley turned away from the fence. "The others will do. Twenty-two dollars apiece for all but my brown, the broken-down sorrel, the outlaw gray, and the mule. That leaves twenty-six head. If my arithmetic's right, that comes to five hundred and seventy-two dollars. We'll make it an even five seventy." He lifted an eyebrow at Brubs. "That set okay with you?"

Brubs scratched a finger into his collar-length hair as if studying on the matter. "Was hopin' for twenty-five."

"I told you I don't dicker, McCallan." Irritation flared in Langley's eyes. "Take it or leave it."

"I reckon five seventy's fair enough, considerin' five or six of the ponies ain't much more than green-broke," Brubs said. "You just bought yourself some horses." He offered a hand. "I usual close a deal by offerin' a man a drink, but me and Dave is fresh out of whiskey." Willoughby heard the hopeful note in Brubs's tone.

Langley stared at the hand for a moment, then took it. He grinned wryly and shook his head. "You are a piece of work, McCallan. You ride in here with a cavvy of thirty horses, most of them likely stolen, try to sell me my own horse, bluff your way out of a hanging, and now you expect me to supply the whiskey, too."

Brubs pumped Langley's hand. "Now that's a right neighborly offer of you, Wes. Right neighborly." He licked his lips as he released Langley's grip. "Old Dave and me sure got bone-dry, trailin' this stock all the way up here."

Langley sighed. "All right, come on up to the house. I've got a bottle there. And your money. I expect a bill of sale on these mounts, just in case someone rides by and recognizes another one as stolen."

Brubs winced. "Now, Wes, there ain't no need to hurt a man's feelin's like that, hintin' we mighta stole them horses. Why, we'll be plumb tickled to give you a bill of sale on ever' blasted one of 'em."

Langley lifted an eyebrow. "That might keep somebody from getting killed. It already has, once. Come along."

Brubs fell into step behind Langley. Willoughby pocketed the papers, lifted his money belt from his saddlebag, and turned to follow. He glanced back at the one-eyed man and felt his belly quiver. If looks could kill, he thought, they'd be dead men right now. He breathed a silent sigh of relief as the ranch house door closed behind him and shut off the icy stare of that one eye.

Langley waved Brubs and Willoughby to seats on benches that flanked a long table in the middle of the main room, then strode to a small desk tucked into a corner. Langley rummaged in the bottom drawer of the desk for a moment, then brought a sheaf of greenbacks, a bottle, and three glasses to the table. He put the money on the table and poured a couple of fingers of whiskey into each of the glasses.

Brubs fondled the currency for a moment, then reached for his liquor glass. He nodded at Willoughby. "My partner here takes care of the cipherin' and stuff for the company. Dave, sign them papers over to Wes."

Willoughby rummaged in a pocket, found a stub of a pencil, and started signing over ownership of the horses in a fine, flowing script.

"It ain't like I was one of them folks can't read and write," Brubs said. "I finished fifth grade, and it didn't take me but three years to get through it. Could have done it in two, but there was too many rabbits to hunt and fish to catch to waste all that time on schoolin'." He sipped at the liquor and sighed in contentment. "Mother's milk to a man dyin' of thirst."

Langley sipped from his glass. "Speaking of dying," he said, "I probably would have hung you two just for the hell of it if you hadn't rode with Stump Hankins."

Brubs downed another swallow. "I sure enough miss that old badger. A good man, that one. Don't make 'em like old Stump no more."

"I heard Gilberto Delgado killed Stump."

Brubs drained his glass and cocked a hopeful eyebrow at the bottle on the table. "That's a pure fact. That damn horse thief's bunch shot poor old Stump near to pieces over at Mustang Mesa. Dave and me tried to stop it, but we was outgunned somethin' fierce."

Wes Langley lifted his glass, swirled the contents for a moment, then tossed the drink back in one swallow. "Story is that you boys went after Delgado."

"Not Delgado personal," Brubs said. "That bad blood between him and Stump wasn't none of our business. But Delgado stole our horses, so we went and stole 'em back."

Langley refilled Brubs's glass. "I didn't figure you two for lace drawers types, but that took some kind of guts. Delgado and his bunch are meaner than wolf poison."

"Wasn't no trouble," Brubs said offhandedly. "Dave, you ain't gonna drink that good whiskey, scoot that glass over this way."

Willoughby stopped writing long enough to sip

33

at the liquor and hoped he hadn't made a mistake. When he got together with Brubs McCallan and whiskey at the same time, bad things started to happen. A few minutes later he handed the horse sale papers to Langley.

Brubs picked up the currency and started stuffing it into Willoughby's money belt. "Aren't you going to count that, McCallan?" Langley asked.

Brubs shook his head and grinned. "I reckon a good honest rancher like you wouldn't cheat a couple of poor workin' hoss traders, Wes," he said.

Willoughby drained his glass and pushed back from the table. He reached for the money belt. "We'd better be on our way, Brubs," he said with a pointed look at the whiskey bottle.

"Yeah, I reckon you're right, partner," Brubs said. "Wouldn't be neighborly to drink up all Wes's whiskey. We can make Austin by supper time." He stood and offered a hand to Wes Langley. "Anytime you're in the market for more good hossflesh, you just get word to us again."

Langley shook Brubs's hand, then Willoughby's. "I'll do that. I'm curious about something, McCallan. Did you really think you two were fast enough to draw on my boys?"

Brubs chuckled aloud. "Hell, no. Old Dave here's slow as February molasses on the draw, and he's a damn sight quicker'n I am. But we woulda given it a try. A good clean shootin' would beat hell out of a hangin'."

"Can't argue with that," Langley said. "By the

way, it might be a good idea to watch out for Hake when you're in these parts. He didn't exactly take a shine to you when he saw that .44 Henry rimfire rifle of yours, McCallan. Hake's a moody sort of fellow. Beat a man half to death down in Goliad a while back. Bit his nose clean off, bone and all. I wouldn't want to tangle with him."

"Neither would we, Mr. Langley," Willoughby said earnestly. "Neither would we."

Dave Willoughby rode in silence at Brubs's side for the better part of an hour, his gut still gurgling over the near hanging at the Slash L. Brubs whistled an off-key tune as happy as a pup with a gravy biscuit, the mule trotting alongside Brubs's sorrel. Looking at Brubs, Willoughby thought, it was as if nothing out of the ordinary had happened at the Langley ranch.

Willoughby yanked at the lead rope of the four-horse string. The sorrel Langley had rejected kept setting back on his haunches, fighting the halter.

Brubs glanced at the balky animal. "That wind-broke sorrel don't lead so good. Probably drag better if you knocked him down." Brubs abruptly checked his mount and grinned at Dave. "Say, partner, how's about we swing by Goliad? They got one hell of a fine saloon down there. And you remember them two sisters —"

Willoughby pulled his black to a stop and glared hard at Brubs for a moment. "You are

35

slap-dab out of your mind, Brubs McCallan. Goliad? In case you've forgotten, there are a bunch of Clantons in Goliad. The man we killed was a Clanton."

"No need to get fretted up about that, Dave. Clanton deserved it. Besides, they don't know who done it."

"How can you be so positive about that?"

" 'Cause old Hake woulda killed us sure if he knowed it for a fact. He didn't."

Willoughby snorted. "He is probably just waiting his turn as a courtesy to all the others lined up to do us in. We aren't going back to Goliad. Once was enough."

Brubs's grin widened. "Boy, we did have us some fun there last time," he said. "You remember them two sisters."

"I certainly do." Dave's voice went tight. "The one I was with was married. To a lawman with a ten-bore shotgun. I barely got out of there without catching a load of buckshot in my backside. We are not going to Goliad."

Brubs's eyes widened. "Why, partner, I didn't know you was so twitchy about one little old town. Trust me. There ain't nothing goin' to happen if we just drop in for a spell."

"Every time you say that, Brubs, I hear the thundering hooves of pestilence, war, famine, and death in my ears."

Brubs shook his head sadly. "There you go again. Always lookin' for some storm cloud in a plumb blue sky. Why, we got us one of them

36

guardian angels ridin' along on our saddle horns."

Willoughby threw his hands in the air in exasperation. *"Felix qui potuit retum cognoscere causas,"* he said.

"There you go with that foreign lingo college stuff again. Talk American."

"It's a quote from Voltaire. It translates as, 'Lucky is he who has been able to understand the causes of things.' "

Brub's brows wrinkled in puzzlement. "I don't follow you, amigo."

"Let us just say, my friend, that since I have met you I have been whipped in a common barroom brawl, thrown in jail, shot at by bandits, stomped by horses, almost drowned, barely escaped from an irate father on one occasion and from a shotgun-wielding husband on another. I have been stabbed by cactus and mesquite thorns and scarred by rope burns. I have been bitten or stung by every fagged and stingered creature known to Texas. I have become a thief and a killer, a wanted fugitive with a price on my head —"

"Twenty-five dollars!" Brubs interrupted with a snort of disgust. "I'm still a mite peeved over that myself, partner. That is the most downright insultin' thing anybody ever done to me. We ought to be worth at least a hundred. That tight-fisted old skinflint —"

"And today I was almost hanged," Willoughby continued, ignoring the interruption. "You have

37

added yet one more variable to the equation you are devising by which to get me killed. To refer back to Voltaire, I am lucky, because I am able now to understand the causes of things. The causes, Brubs McCallan, are — in ascending order — you and liquor, you and money, you and women, and you."

A wide grin slowly spread across Brubs's stubbled face. "Yep, amigo, we have had us a passel of fun, at that. You sure had me goin' there for a minute. I thought you was on the prod about somethin'."

Dave glowered ominously at Brubs. "For the last and final time, we are not — repeat, *not* — going into Goliad."

"Must be Saturday," Brubs said as he reined the sorrel onto the main street of the small but bustling community. "Never seen this many folks in Goliad before."

Willoughby yanked irritably on the lead rope as the sorrel tried to balk again. "They probably came for the hanging," he grumbled.

Brubs lifted an eyebrow quizzically. "Didn't hear nothin' about no hangin' today."

"I was talking about ours. Or at least the probability thereof." Willoughby snorted. "I will never understand why I let you talk me into one pickle barrel after another. You missed your calling, Brubs. You should have been a snake oil salesman."

Brubs kneed Squirrel out of the path of a shiny

new buggy and tipped his hat to a pretty girl on the seat beside a broad-shouldered and surly-looking man. "See there, Dave?" Brubs said as the buggy rolled past. "This here little town's just runnin' over with cute fillies. Let's get these horses stabled and go hunt us up a bottle and a couple prime females."

Willoughby pulled his horse to a stop. "Wait a minute! You promised all we were going to do was buy supplies and sell these animals Langley didn't want. You swore we wouldn't be going into any saloons or whorehouses."

"Now, partner," Brubs said, a pained expression on his sun-browned face, "I said you wouldn't have to go in no saloon if you wasn't of a mind to. Didn't promise none such about me. Besides, you was the one all hot and bothered for a bath and a shave, not me."

"Anybody riding on the downwind side of you would know that," Willoughby grumbled. "I am not going to turn you loose in a bar with our hard-earned horse money."

"Just a few dollars is all I need, Dave. You know there ain't no real cowboy waterin' holes between here and LaQuesta. One little drink or two to cut the trail dust won't hurt nothin'."

"When you say something won't hurt I can already feel the pain." Dave's shoulders slumped in resignation. "Brubs McCallan, you know full well I'll have to go along and ride herd on you or we'll be broke by sunup."

Brubs said, "Now, that's what I call a real

partner. Let's stable these horses and tree us a town" — he raised a hand to ward off Willoughby's protest — "but we'll tree her sort of quiet-like. Why, I'll be plumb gentlemanly about it."

Willoughby jabbed a finger at him. "Before you go into any saloon, we're buying the supplies we need to get back to LaQuesta. Then we are going to get baths and shaves."

Brubs sighed and shock his head. "I swear, Dave, I never saw a man so fretty over a few whiskers and a little bit o' trail dust."

"That's the deal. Take it, as Wes Langley said, or leave it." Willoughby yanked on the lead rope and kneed his black toward the town livery a block away.

Brubs reined in alongside. "Partner, you get plumb et up with sour sometimes. You got to learn to rear back and have some fun before I can make a genuine Texan out of you."

Willoughby shot a caustic glance at Brubs. "What worries me," he said, "is that someday you just might. If I live that long."

Dave Willoughby was feeling half human again. A bath, a shave, and a new set of clothes always had a soothing effect on him. Goliad's Lone Star Saloon had a familiar smell to it, the scent of sawdust, man sweat, tobacco smoke, and stale beer.

He leaned against the bar and sipped from the neck of his beer bottle. The brew was good, a bit on the malty side for his taste, but it was cool. At his side, Brubs had already lowered the level of a four-dollar bottle of Old Overholt by a third, but Brubs's eyes were still clear and his words weren't slurred.

As usual, Brubs's tongue was flapping. He had an animated conversation going with a man in a derby hat and an expensive hand-tailored silk suit. Probably a merchant, banker, or some such, Willoughby figured. At least Brubs hadn't started anything dangerous yet. Willoughby began to relax. Maybe this time trouble would pass them by.

He picked up his beer bottle and turned to survey the dimly lit interior. His gaze fell on a perky brunette woman who had a hip perched on a nearby table, talking with a customer. She was barely five feet tall, but certainly well equipped for her trade. Her gaze caught his; Willoughby saw the invitation, the flash of interest, in her dark eyes, and felt the skin of his neck flush. He had never understood why women seemed drawn to him. He was uncomfortable around women. Especially whores. He could never think of the right words. He turned back to the bar, sipped at his beer, and tried to put the brunette from his mind. A few more minutes, and he and Brubs would be on the trail back to LaQuesta and home. . . .

"McCallan!"

The bellow spun Willoughby around. His heart dropped to the pit of his stomach.

41

A big man with one eye stood just inside the door, his bulk almost blacking out the rectangle of light.

Brubs turned casually to face the big man. "Howdy, Hake," he said. "Buy you a drink?"

"You sawed-off little bastard!" The roar of the big man's voice seemed to shake the globes on the oil lamps flanking the bar. "I'm calling you out, damn you! What's it going to be — guns, knives, or fists?"

THREE

The sudden silence in the Lone Star Saloon was almost deafening.

Willoughby felt the quickened hammering of his heart against his rib cage. He was sure everyone in the place could hear the solid thumps in the smoky air.

The man called Hake stood in the doorway, the sunlight framing his big body and glittering off the steel back strap of the revolver at his belt and the haft of a heavy bladed knife sheathed opposite the pistol.

Willoughby glanced at Brubs. The stocky Texan leaned against the bar, a glass in one hand. The bartender stood halfway between Willoughby and Brubs, a damp rag forgotten in his hand. The tick of a heavy mantel clock seemed as loud as church bells in the thick silence.

It was Brubs McCallan who finally shattered the quiet.

"Hake, I've heard friendlier greetin's before." Brubs's tone was unconcerned, almost jocular. "Come on in and shut the door. You're lettin' all the flies out."

Hake limped forward, his footsteps heavy on the hardwood floor. The door slammed behind him. In the dim light of the saloon, Willoughby could see the glitter of rage in the one brown eye. The white scar stood out in sharp relief against the deep brown of Hake's twisted face.

"Looks like somethin' got your frumps up today, Hake," Brubs said casually. "Piles actin' up on you again?"

"You sawed-off little runt, I come to kill you." Hake's voice was not a bellow this time; it was quiet, controlled, and more menacing than the earlier roar.

Brubs lifted his glass. "You got some reason to do that?"

"Damn right I have. You're a liar, a horse thief, a bushwhacker, and an all-around bastard to boot."

Brubs sipped at his drink, then lowered his glass. "Well now," he said, "I reckon I spun some windies in my time. I ain't sayin' I did or didn't, but I mighta borrowed a horse once or twice. And I sure can't argue I ain't a bastard. I never seen my pa." He put the glass on the bar. "But, friend, I ain't no bushwhacker. Never killed a man that I didn't look him in the eye first."

"I'm looking you in the eye right now, McCallan," Hake growled. "Reckon you're stud hoss enough to take me?"

Brubs half grinned. "Maybe. If I was a mind to." He hefted the half empty bottle from the bar. "Simmer down Hake. Have yourself a snort of Old Skullbuster. You can apologize later for callin' me a bushwhacker."

Willoughby thought Hake's one good eye was about to pop from his head. "Damn your soul, McCallan! You ain't gonna weasel out of this! I

44

called you out! So what'll it be — guns, knives, or fists?"

Brubs casually poured himself another drink and tossed it back in one swallow. "Hake, you just won't quit, will you?" He sighed heavily. "I got to give you credit for offerin' a near fair fight, I reckon."

"Quit yammering, dammit! Get on with it! What's your pleasure?"

Brubs's brows furrowed as if in deep thought. "Can't say pistols. Dave here's too fast for you —"

"Brubs!" Willoughby's voice was a surprised croak.

"And besides, sometimes he just gets plumb carried away, crazy-like, shoots anything that moves, and we don't want no innocent folks hit. Knives?" Brubs shook his head. "Nah. Too messy. Dave don't cotton much to knife fights. Why, the last man knife-fought Dave bled smooth to death, and they wasn't a cut on him deeper'n an inch."

"Brubs —"

"Hush up, Dave," Brubs said. "I know you ain't got much patience when you're pushed, but can't you see I'm tryin' to make this easier for you?"

"Me?"

Brubs waved a hand. "Relax, partner. I'm thinkin' here." He was silent for a moment, then shook his head. "Fists won't do, neither. Can't take a chance on Dave bustin' his shootin' hand. Besides, the last man he beat to death was a long time dyin'. Hammered his kidneys plumb to pieces. Poor feller peed blood nigh on to a month." He sighed. "Anyhow, fistfights bust up saloons. Never could see wreckin' a fine community service place like this, could it be avoided."

Hake glanced from Brubs to Willoughby and back again his forehead wrinkled. "Just what the hell are you trying to pull here, McCallan?" Hake's voice still held its menacing rumble, but now it was touched by confusion.

"I'd like to know that myself, Brubs," Willoughby said. The knot in his gut drew itself tighter. He was afraid he was going to find out the answer. It wasn't reassuring.

Brubs flashed a disarming grin at the big man, then reached out and clapped a hand against the shoulder of the man in the silk suit and derby hat. "Hake, this here's Daniel C. Thornton, from Houston. Lawyer by trade."

Thornton wavered slightly on his feet as he inclined his head in a greeting. The lawyer looked like a man who had just put away the better part of a quart of bourbon. Which he had.

"Lawyer?" The wrinkles in Hake's forehead deepened.

Brubs poured a hefty dollop of whiskey into a glass and handed it to Hake. "Have a shot while Daniel C. and me works this out, Hake. We're gonna try to make it as easy on you as possible." Brubs turned to Thornton. "What's the law on duels?"

"Dueling has been outlawed in Texas since Sam Houston's time," Thornton said, his words slurred a bit.

"Before then. This here feller challenged me. Ain't I got the choice of weapons?" He cut a quick glance at Hake. "Drink up, Hake. This may take a minute."

Hake lifted the glass.

Thornton's brow wrinkled in thought for a moment. "The challenged has the right to choice of weapons and field of battle, best I can recall."

Brubs refilled Hake's glass. "Daniel C., is there any duelin' rule says I can't choose *two* weapons?"

"You mean, as in swords and pistols both?" At Brubs's nod, Thornton downed another quick shot of bourbon. "I suppose that would be acceptable. If it wasn't illegal. Which it is."

Brubs's grin stretched wider. "Well, by God, there you have it. Hake, I done picked my number one weapon — Mr. Dave Willoughby here."

"What! Brubs, dammit —"

"Settle down, Dave. Don't get yourself in no rush to kill this poor unsuspectin' cripple. Just look at him — he ain't got but one good eye, and a bum leg on top of that. I'm just tryin' to find some way to even things out for old Hake, so's he ain't at too much of a disadvantage and still let him keep his manly honor."

Hake looked more confused than ever.

"Brubs —"

"Hush up, Dave. I'm thinkin'." Brubs snapped his fingers. "By God, I got it!"

"What?" Hake's forehead furrowed deeper.

"Tequila."

"What?" Hake sounded completely befuddled.

"My second weapon, Hake. The sure 'nuff Texan way to settle a dispute." Brubs reached out and cuffed the big man on the shoulder, raising a puff of dust. "Now, Hake, you look big enough to drink a barrel of the stuff and not never feel it. You take a look at old Dave here. Why, he ain't but skin and bones. Don't hardly throw a shadow on a bright day."

"What the hell?" Hake's eyebrows almost met. He shook his head.

"Here's what we do, Hake." Brubs's tone gained excitement as he warmed to the idea. "We set you and Dave down at one of these here tables — that's my field of battle — with a bottle of tequila. Match shot for shot, straight. First man to pass out loses. Course, Hake, if you're afraid you can't outdrink that skinny feller, I reckon we'll have to go back to the guns or knives stuff —"

"Damn your hide, McCallan!" Anger flared anew in Hake's eye. "I can drink any man alive under the table!"

Brubs winked at Willoughby over Hake's shoulder. "That's what I figured, Hake. Why, you're half alligator and half grizzly bear when it comes to drinkin', I'd bet. Now, what we got to do is find us a impartial referee, like in prizefights." He glanced around the room. Willoughby's gaze followed his. Brubs's eyes settled on the shapely brunette. "Say, missy, what's your name?"

"Missy," she said with a toothy smile.

"How's about you be the referee? You call a foul if one of 'em tries to skip a round or don't down the whole shot." He plucked a bill from his shirt pocket and handed it to the girl. "Your fee, Missy. You just make sure there ain't no cheatin'."

Willoughby tugged frantically at Brubs's sleeve. "What the hell are you doing, McCallan?" he whispered urgently. "Trying to kill me with alcohol poisoning?"

"Dave," Brubs whispered back, "we both know this man would tear you into little bitty pieces in a fistfight. You can't hardly gut a lizard with a knife, and you sure as hell can't shoot. I'm tryin' my best to save your life here." Brubs's lower lip protruded in a wounded pout. "Least you could do is show a little appreciation."

"*You* are trying to save *my* life? Brubs, I think I'm missing something here."

"Look, Dave, we can't lose. Even if he did beat you which I don't think he can, he'd be so damn drunk he wouldn't be able to hurt you."

"And, I suppose, he will be in no condition to hurt *you,* either. Which seems to be the reason he came here in the first place."

"I ain't worried, partner. I seen you work a tequila bottle down in Chihuahua at Tres Perros.

49

You was still standin' when the rest of us was down, and you didn't even have no hangover next mornin'. It's like you don't feel no poison from the tequila tarantula. If you can drink me under the table, you can sure as hell take this big guy. Course, if you'd rather fight him —"

"Oh, Christ," Willoughby moaned softly. "Bring on the damn bottle. If I've got to die, at least I'll go without feeling any pain." He paused long enough to pin an icy glare on Brubs. "And when it's over, Brubs McCallan, I may just decide to whip your butt myself."

Brubs said, "Now you're talkin', Dave. Matter of fact, I think we can make us some money out of this. Gimme a couple of those big bills out of the Slash L horse money." Brubs turned to the circle of customers that had gathered around. "I'm puttin' twenty bucks on this tall skinny guy bein' the last one standin'. Any takers?"

By the time the first bottle arrived, saloon customers stood eight deep around the table, their fists full of money. Most of the bets went down on Hake. The brunette called Missy carefully poured two shot glasses full to the rim from the tequila bottle. She raised her hand.

Dave Willoughby looked deep into the one brown eye across the table. The big man still looked confused. Willoughby knew exactly how he felt. The brunette said, "Go," and dropped her hand.

Willoughby picked up the shot glass and downed the contents in one gulp. Hake did the same. A mutter went up from the crowd, then a cheer, about the same time the tequila shot hit Willoughby's belly and exploded. Missy refilled the glasses.

"Willoughby," Hake said, his eye watering from the shock of the raw liquor, "I ain't sure just what happened here to get in the way of a good fight, but I know one thing — that man you ride with is one strange hombre."

Willoughby lifted his glass. "You aren't telling me a thing I don't already know, Hake." He downed the shot.

"Dave? Partner, you all right?"

Willoughby came half awake and instantly regretted it. Every thump of his heart sent a bolt of agony through his temples, every breath jabbed a pain through his rib cage. His eyes felt like a bunch of kids were playing mumblety-peg with a dull knife behind the sockets. It seemed to him that even his hair hurt.

Brubs poked Willoughby's shoulder again. "Dave?"

"Go away," he mumbled. "Lemma die." The words were croaky, slurred by a tongue that seemed to have grown fur — from the south end of a northbound rabbit. He struggled to focus his eyes and could see nothing but a hazy brownish blur. It slowly dawned on him that he was lying facedown in the dirt.

"Come on, partner," Brubs said, "let's see what's left of you."

51

Willoughby thought Brubs's voice sounded funny. But there was nothing funny about this morning. He felt a hand slip under his shoulder. Brubs hauled him to a sitting position in the trash-littered alley. The movement made the buildings lean and start to spin. Willoughby closed his eyes, waiting for the dizziness to pass.

"Dave, son, you look like hell."

Willoughby cracked one eye open. Brubs squatted beside him. The stocky Texan had a smear of blood on one temple and a knot the size of a hen's egg above his left eye. "You are truly a comfort to a dying man, Brubs," Willoughby managed to croak. Even his throat was sore. "What happened?"

"You don't recollect?"

"Wouldn't have asked if I did." Willoughby tried to open both eyes and wound up squinting against the early morning sunlight that streamed over one of the buildings. The light made the mumblety-peg game in his skull more intense. A yellow cur dog trotted down the alley, stopped to sniff at Willoughby's boot, then hoisted its leg. "Go ahead," Willoughby mumbled at the dog, "everybody else does."

Brubs whapped the dog on the ear with his hat. The mongrel yelped and ran away, its tail between its legs.

"Dave, I never seen you with a sure-'nuff hangover before," Brubs said. "Reckon now I'll get a tad more sympathy when I'm in that shape."

Willoughby's stomach churned. "I never had

a real headbuster before. Don't plan to do it again. If I live. Now, what happened?"

"Startin' when?"

"Last thing I remember is Missy cracking that third bottle."

"Oh, yeah. We run out of tequila along about then. Most likely that's how come you don't feel so hot this mornin'. Had to switch to gin."

Willoughby moaned aloud. "Gin! God, I hate gin. I get queasy every time I smell a juniper bush." He wiped a hand across his forehead. It came away sweaty and streaked with alley dirt. "Who won?"

"You did, amigo," Brubs said cheerfully. "Made me plumb proud. Old Hake passed out halfway through that second gin jug. Just plopped facedown on the table. Ain't seen him since. Reckon you can stand up?"

"Don't want to. Rather die sitting down. Don't have that far to fall."

Brubs cuffed him playfully on the shoulder. "Dave, you ain't gonna die. The Creator don't call a man home till he's paid his dues for the night before." Brubs rubbed the back of his own neck. "I'm payin' a bit myself this mornin'. I had to cheer my partner on. Went through most of a bottle givin' you moral support."

Willoughby turned a bleary gaze on Brubs. "I didn't know your purity of innocence had been tainted by morals McCallan." He heaved himself erect and leaned against the wall until the world got its feet back under it. He lifted a shaky hand

and ran a palm over the stubble on his chin. The scratching sound was painfully loud in his ears. He noticed the fresh scrapes and bruises on his knuckles and stared for a moment at his hand. "How did that happen?"

Brubs said, "It was after you went upstairs with Missy."

"After I what?"

"Dave, son, don't you remember?"

"No."

"Well, I swan." Brubs shook his head in sympathy. "Man ought to recall somethin' like that Missy. Prime filly, she is. Anyway, you come back downstairs after about a half hour, brayin' at the moon about how you could whup any two men in the place —"

"Good God! *I* said *that?*"

"Sure did. Turns out you couldn't. Dave, if I was you I wouldn't go mixin' tequila and gin no more." Brubs sucked at his own skinned knuckles. "We give it a helluva try, though. Thought we was gonna get her done there for a while, till somebody laid most of a chair upside my head. Don't remember nothin' after that, myself."

Willoughby sagged against the rough stucco wall and pressed a hand against aching ribs. His eyes snapped fully open. "Brubs — the money belt. It's gone."

Brubs shrugged. "Been thinkin' I ought to talk to you about that, partner. I took it for safe keepin' when you went upstairs with Missy. Can't trust these small-town whores you know.

54

Well, things started gettin' a little hazy not long after that. When I come to a while back in this alley, the belt was gone."

"You mean to tell me we were robbed?"

"Rolled and robbed like a greenhorn in Abilene," Brubs said casually. "Damn shame, too. I'd built that poke up to near eight hundred dollars bettin' on you to drink old Hake under the table."

Willoughby moaned aloud. "Eight hundred dollars. Two months' worth of work. Gone."

Brubs chuckled aloud. "Maybe so, but we sure had us a good time, partner."

"Eight hundred dollars' worth?"

Brubs pushed away from the wall. "You fret too much over nonsensical things. Money's just somethin' a man trades for a little fun now and again. It ain't like we was flat broke anyway, partner. I got a double eagle snuck back in my boot. Them two horses we brung along ought to be worth another fifteen apiece, and the mule twenty. We got us some good saddle horses and plenty of grub. Hell, we are nigh on to rich by Texas standards, and I done figured out how we can make more money easy enough."

Willoughby raised an aching eyebrow. "I'm afraid to ask."

"We know a rich grandee down in Sonora who's short of horses. We know he's short of horses on account of we was the ones who shorted him. And Texas is full of horses."

"Wait a minute — you mean to steal horses

55

here and sell them to a man we've already stolen others from? You can't be serious."

Brubs's mustache twitched. "Never been seriouser."

Willoughby's shoulders slumped. *"Si possis recte, si non, quocumue modo rem."*

"Talk American."

"Horace said that. Sort of the motto of our business partnership, I suppose. It means, 'If possible honestly, if not, somehow make money.' "

Brubs said, "By golly, that Horace character woulda made a right fine Texan." His smile slowly faded. "I reckon we might ought to saddle up and get a move on, Dave. Better scout out horse herds in another part of the country, on account of it could get a little chancy for us around Goliad. Heard talk last night that a couple of them Clanton boys was comin' into town today."

Willoughby stared silently at Brubs for a couple of heartbeats. "You are just full of sunshine and good news this morning, you know that?" He pushed himself away from the wall and tried to ignore the stabbing pain in his temples. "If you're waiting on me, you're wasting time."

Brubs McCallan leaned back against the fallen trunk of a big cottonwood tree, coffee cup in hand, and watched the first gold wash of dawn paint the sky of the wooded ridge overlooking the campsite in a clearing on the Pedernales

River. He patted his stomach in contentment and listened to the faint scratching sounds as Dave Willoughby dragged a straight razor across the stubble on his cheek.

This, Brubs decided, was the best camp yet. They were three days out of Goliad, scouting the countryside in a wide circle around San Antonio. Somebody there might remember old man Lawrence T. Pettibone putting that reward on their heads, and there were folks who thought twenty-five dollars was a heap of money. They had found no horse ranches worth raiding that weren't owned by honest folks or guarded by ornery-looking men with big guns, but Brubs didn't mind. He was enjoying the ride.

The morning air was still, comfortably cool, and awash in bird songs from the groves of trees lining the river on three sides of the camp. A whitetail doe topped the ridge a hundred yards east and stood outlined against the rapidly brightening sky. Brubs thought about reaching for his rifle, but almost immediately abandoned the idea. They still had bacon and jerked beef in the possibles sack and nearly sixty cash dollars in the saddlebags that lay across the dead tree trunk near his shoulder. There was no need to shoot the deer. The doe was a dainty little thing, anyway. Sort of reminded Brubs of that red-haired gal up in Denton. He sighed in wistful memory. The redhead hadn't been the least bit dainty between the sheets. He watched until the deer dropped her head and disappeared over the ridge, then lifted his cup in a salute to Willoughby.

"You're a mighty good hand with a skillet, partner," Brubs said. "You'll make some lucky gal a fine wife one of these days. Marry you myself, was you put together proper."

"Wouldn't have you if I was," Willoughby said. He held the razor up. "I don't suppose you want to use this before I put it away?"

Brubs shook his head. "There ain't no women around. I swear, I can't figure what you got against whiskers. Maybe your ma got scared by a billy goat before you was born." He drained the last of his coffee and tossed the empty cup to Willoughby. "Darn near daylight and not a lick of work done yet, partner. I'll saddle the horses whilst you tidy up the camp. Which one you want today?"

"Choctaw."

Brubs sang a slightly off-key and thoroughly off-color saloon ditty as he strode to the pickets where the horses waited at the edge of a stand of cottonwood, oak, and pecan trees. He saddled Mouse, the gray mustang, then heaved Willoughby's rig onto the leggy roan. He was reaching for the latigo strap when the yell came:

"Brubs, watch out!"

A split second later Brubs heard the meaty slap of a slug against flesh and the crack of a rifle. He spun toward the camp.

Willoughby was down.

FOUR

Brubs had only a fleeting glimpse of Willoughby lying beside the camp fire before the big roan spooked at the sudden crack of the rifle shot. Choctaw jumped sideways, pinning Brubs against the gray mustang for an instant and almost squeezing the air from his lungs.

Brubs instinctively whipped Dave's Winchester from the saddle scabbard as Choctaw lunged away. He eared back the hammer of the rifle and snapped a shot toward a puff of gun smoke from the top of the ridge. A startled yelp sounded; an instant later a slug cracked past Brubs's ear. He threw himself to the ground, rolled free of the tangle of hooves as the horses fought the tethers, and racked a fresh round into the .44-40. He glanced at the still form by the camp fire. A slug kicked dirt beside Willoughby's head.

"Dave!"

His yell went unanswered. Dave did not move.

Brubs levered two quick shots into a bloom of powder smoke from the edge of the trees at his left and heard the satisfying whack of lead on flesh and a choked grunt. He scrambled to his feet; a slug kicked sand beside his left boot. Brubs snapped another round toward the muzzle flash, then sprinted toward the still figure on the sand, weaving as he ran. Lead snapped the air beside his head and splapped into the trees behind the clearing. Brubs shifted the Winchester to his left hand, grabbed Willoughby's collar with his right, and dragged the unconscious man toward the thick tree trunk lying a few feet away. He felt a light blow against his left shoulder just as he dropped behind the deadfall.

The gunfire abruptly stopped.

Brubs crouched at Willoughby's side. A red stain spread over the left side of his partner's shirt just above the belt; his breath came in shallow, ragged gasps. His eyes were closed. Brubs glanced at his own shoulder. The cloth of his shirt was torn. Blood trickled from a shallow bullet track and dribbled down the upper part of his left arm. He felt no pain.

"You in the camp!" The yell from the trees was clear in the still morning air. "Might as well come on out! We got you pinned down!"

Brubs didn't reply. He studied the heavy timber, trying to pinpoint the source of the calls. He could see no movement. The shots had come from different rifles, one on the ridge and one in the trees. That meant there were at least two men out there.

"McCallan! We saw your partner go down! No use in you getting killed, too!"

Brubs glanced at Willoughby. The lean face was pale, twisted in pain, the eyes still closed. "Hang in there, friend," Brubs whispered, "we ain't dead yet." He knew Willoughby was hit hard. He was going to need help, and soon. Brubs peered over the top of the deadfall, squinting against the rising sun. He saw nothing but shapes and shadows. He knew he had to make a move soon, before the bushwhackers decided to flank the camp, come up behind, and plop some lead between his shoulder blades. Brubs became aware of the growing sting from the bullet crease along his upper arm. The initial cold jolt of fear and surprise at the dawn ambush gave way to a growing ember of rage in his gut.

"McCallan! Give us your money and horses and we'll call it even! We'll let you walk away!"

"In a pig's butt, you will," Brubs muttered aloud. He forced himself to calmly study out his position. They were in a sort of standoff, at least for now. The attackers couldn't rush the camp without exposing themselves to his rifle. He couldn't get to the horses without drawing fire. And Dave Willoughby didn't have the time to wait out any sort of siege. The wounded man moaned softly. Brubs made his decision. It was chancy, but it was all he had.

"Give it up, McCallan, or we're coming in!"

"Hold up a minute!" Brubs yelled back. "I'm thinkin' on it! My partner's hurt real bad!" He eased his hand into the near side pouch of the saddlebag. His fingers closed on the grips of the spare Colt, an old .45 taken from the body of a dead bandit. It was the same Colt that had killed Jake Clanton. Brubs slipped it from the saddlebag, checked to make sure it was loaded, cocked the weapon, and placed it beside his right knee. "All right!" Brubs yelled. "Money's in these sad-

61

dlebags! It's yours! Just let me and my partner go!"

After a moment's silence from the trees, the call came back: "Throw the bags out! Then your guns!" The voice sounded closer now.

Brubs hesitated, calculating the odds. He would have just one chance. He glanced at Willoughby and knew that was one more chance than Dave would have if they didn't get out of this trap soon. He steeled himself, pulled the saddlebags from the trunk, and heaved them toward the camp fire.

"Now the guns!"

Brubs tossed out Willoughby's rifle, then their two pistol belts. "Leave us one horse!" Brubs called. "My partner's shot bad!"

"Lift your hands, McCallan!"

Brubs raised his hands to shoulder height. For several heartbeats, nothing moved along the trees or on the slope of the eastern ridge. Then a stocky, barrel-chested man emerged from the shadows, rifle at the ready. A taller, lean man followed, limping heavily, his left thigh dark with blood. The gunmen moved warily at first, then seemed to relax. The stocky one strode straight to the saddlebags and picked them up in his right hand.

The tall man knelt to scoop up Willoughby's pistol belt. For an instant, both gunmen were distracted. Brubs swept the cocked Colt from beside his knee.

"I got a question for you boys," Brubs said

casually. "How do you plan to get out of that clearin' alive?"

The thin man yelped, dropped Willoughby's gun belt, and started to shoulder his rifle. Brubs squeezed the trigger. The .45 slug hammered into the thin man's belly. He dropped his rifle, staggered back a step, and went down. Brubs swung the Colt's muzzle to the stocky man, thumbed the hammer, and fired. The man's body jerked under the impact, but he didn't go down. The big man lifted a hand to his chest, looked at the bloody palm in disbelief, then dropped his rifle. "You nailed me hard, McCallan. Don't shoot no more."

"Mister," Brubs said calmly, "you done bit off more biscuit than you can chew when you bush-whacked my partner." He lined the sights and squeezed the trigger. The stocky man's head snapped back as the slug slammed into his fore-head. The impact knocked him sprawling onto his back. Brubs knew he was dead before he hit the ground.

He strode to the lean gunman's side, the Colt cocked and ready. The man wasn't dead yet, but he wasn't feeling too frisky. Brubs relieved the man of his weapons and heaved them as far as he could toward the river.

"I — I'm hit bad," the thin man pleaded, his voice weak. "You got . . . to . . . help me."

Brubs's jaw was still clenched in cold rage as he glared at the downed gunman. "You'll get just as much help from me as you were gonna

63

give me and my partner over there. Which is none." He stared at the man through narrowed lids. "Who the hell are you?"

"Name's . . . Clanton. Ed Clanton." Bloody spittle spotted the corners of the man's thin lips. "We've been . . . following you two . . . since Goliad." He coughed. The thin body convulsed in a fresh blast of agony. He squinted through watery eyes at Brubs. "I got to know . . . for sure. You kill Jake Clanton?"

Brubs nodded. "Bastard deserved it. He wasn't too bright. He didn't figure us for a hide-out gun, either. Dumb seems to run in your family, mister." He turned on a heel and strode away.

"For God's sake — help me." The reedy voice was even thinner in Brubs's ears. "I'm hurtin' . . . awful bad."

"I can't tell you how much that tickles me, Ed," Brubs said over his shoulder as he gathered their weapons and saddlebags and strode back to Willoughby's side. Willoughby's eyes fluttered open.

"What —"

"Easy, partner," Brubs said softly, "you took a slug in the side." He pulled Willoughby's shirt up and peered at the wound. It didn't look good.

"Gut — gut-shot?"

Brubs understood the note of raw fear in Willoughby's voice. He had seen gut-shot men before. It was a brutal damn way to die. "Can't tell, Dave. I reckon the slug's still in there. No hole where it come out. I got to stop the

64

bleedin'." He slipped an arm under Willoughby's shoulders and helped him sit up. Willoughby's breath came in sharp whistles of pain at the movement.

Brubs stripped the bandanna from his neck and worked his belt free. He wadded the cloth against the hole in Willoughby's side and cinched it in place with the belt. "Reckon you can ride, partner?"

"Don't suppose . . . I have a choice," Willoughby said through clenched teeth.

"It'll work out, amigo. Fredericksburg's got a doc. That ain't but five, six hours ride from here."

"You are . . . a pure comfort to a man . . . Brubs McCallan. A pure comfort."

Brubs forced a reassuring grin. "You're grumpin' again. I reckon that's a good sign. I'll fetch the horses."

He paused on the way back from the picket line for a cursory glance at the wounded gunman. Ed Clanton had only a few hours left on this earth, Brubs figured, but they'd be mighty long hours to Ed. Clanton writhed in agony on the sandy soil, hands pressed helplessly against his stomach. "Water — God's sake. Gimme water." Clanton's voice was barely audible.

"I reckon not," Brubs said casually. "I'm in kind of a hurry. You start crawlin' now, you can get to the river by sundown, maybe."

Tears pooled in Clanton's eyes. "Damn you — to hell, McCallan."

"Most likely I'll get there, Ed," Brubs said. "Keep the beer cold for me, will you?"

Twenty minutes later Brubs rode at Willoughby's stirrup, the packhorses trailing behind on loose lead. Willoughby wavered in the saddle; at times his eyes closed and his chin sagged against his chest. His face was almost chalk-white and flowing sweat despite the lingering cool of the early morning.

"Hang in there, partner," Brubs said softly. "I ain't gonna let you die on me now. Not after all the work I put in tryin' to make a real genuine Texan out of you."

One of Willoughby's eyelids cracked open. "I am not going to die on you, dammit." His voice was growing weaker. "I will not give you the satisfaction of finally succeeding in your obsession to get me killed."

Brubs said, "Sounds like you're already feelin' better. Us Texans always say that a bitchin' cowboy is a happy man. It's when they don't talk that a man's gotta worry about 'em."

"That will . . . never apply to you, Brubs McCallan. I never . . . heard a man talk so much." Dave paused to take a ragged breath, winced, and turned a pain-glazed eye to Brubs. "Heard shooting. What happened?"

Brubs shrugged. "Nothin' much. I cut a couple culls out of the Clanton herd while you was snoozin'. Now, quit your infernal yammerin' and ride easy, partner."

Willoughby moaned at a fresh lance of pain.

"Just where was that . . . guardian angel of yours . . . today when we needed her?"

Brubs shook his head. "She's a fickle slut at that, I reckon. She's probably waitin' for us at Helen Richter's place. If Helen don't shotgun the both of us on sight."

Brubs McCallan sat on the hard, straight-backed wooden chair at Helen Richter's kitchen table, shoulders slumped in exhaustion and worry.

For the last ten miles of the long ride from the Pedernales to the small farmhouse outside Fredericksburg, Brubs had had to hold Dave Willoughby in the saddle. Now he had done all he could do — except wait.

He had been afraid that Helen Richter might turn them away, and that if she did Dave might not live the two miles into Fredericksburg proper. His worry had been for nothing. The widow Richter clucked and fluttered around Willoughby like a mother hen, shook her head in dismay at Brubs's crude attempts at bandaging, and promptly put Willoughby to rest in her own bed.

Brubs stood as the bedroom door swung open. A burly, blond man with dark blue eyes strode into the kitchen wiping oversized hands on a bloodstained rag. "How is he, Doc?" Brubs said.

"He should live if there is no serious infection and if his fever breaks in the next few days." The doctor's voice carried a thick German accent. "He lost a lot of blood, but I don't think any intestines were damaged. I was able to get the bullet out. Helen is with him now."

Brubs breathed an audible sigh of relief. "Thanks, Doc. That's mighty good news."

The physician shrugged thick, heavy shoulders. He looked more like a blacksmith than a saw-bones, Brubs thought. "I said he *should* live, not that he *would*," he said, "but he is young, strong, and in good physical condition. If there is no blood poisoning, the odds are in his favor. Slightly." He strode to Brubs and peered over half-moon spectacles at his shoulder. "Let's have a look at that."

Brubs shrugged. "It ain't but a little scratch. Don't even sting much now."

"There is no such thing as a small bullet wound, just as there is no such thing as being partly pregnant." The doctor squinted at the crease, then grunted and left the room. He returned a moment later, a scarred black leather bag in his big hand. "A bit of alcohol and carbolic should take care of it. Not deep enough to need stitches." He pulled a couple of bottles and a cotton swab from the bag. "This may sting just a bit."

"Doc," Brubs said hopefully, "ain't a man sup-posed to have a drink of whiskey before somethin' like this?"

"Good idea," the physician said. He reached into the black bag, pulled out a pint bottle, twisted the cap off and took a long swallow. He screwed the cap back on and stowed the bottle back in the bag with a satisfied sigh.

"That ain't," Brubs said, "exactly what I had in mind." He took a deep breath. "All right, get on with it." He yelped out loud at the fiery touch of the swab. "*May* sting a little? Doc, you got a way of understatin' things just a tad." He ground his teeth as the fire in his shoulder peaked. "Damn, that stuff'd make a man catch a rabbit, sure enough."

The physician finished cleaning the shallow gouge and stowed his medicine bottles back in the bag. "Keep it clean," he said, wrinkling his nose, "if soap and water are not against your religion, as they appear to be. It wouldn't hurt you to shave, either."

"Now what in thunderation has whiskers got to do with a bullet crease, Doc?"

"I wasn't thinking of you. I had Mrs. Richter's best interest in mind. Your friend is going to be here for some time, if he lives — and you, Mr. McCallan, are a bit less than fragrant."

Brubs sniffed in wounded indignation. "I done had a bath, not hardly a whole week ago. You got a mean streak in you, Doc." He sighed. "All right, I'll clean up some." He reached into his pocket. "Much obliged for takin' care of Dave. How much I owe you?"

"Five dollars for now." The doctor waited as Brubs counted a handful of coins, then dropped the money in his shirt pocket. "I'll be back to check on your friend in three or four days. If his fever doesn't break within forty-eight hours, send

69

for me." He picked up his bag and started for the door.

"Doc, if Dave don't get over the fever by then, what'll you do for him?"

The answer chilled Brubs's bones. "Sign his death certificate. I am also," the doctor said, "the county coroner."

Brubs came awake with a start. He sat for a moment, battling the uncomfortable feeling he was being watched.

He was.

Dave Willoughby's eyes were open, and even in the weak light from the bedside lantern Brubs could see that the eyes were no longer glazed with fever.

"Mornin', sunshine," Brubs said. "Feel up to choosin' some prime fillies tonight?"

"How long have I been here?"

Brubs shrugged. "Two, goin' on three days, I reckon. Kind of lost track of time myself. Musta dozed off." He heaved himself stiffly from the hard wooden chair by Willoughby's bedside. "How long you been awake this time, partner?"

"Few minutes." Willoughby stirred under the sheets and grimaced in pain at the movement. "What do you mean, this time?"

Brubs shrugged. "You been in and out of it ever since you got shot. Mostly out of it." He reached out and put a hand against Willoughby's forehead. It was cool to the touch. "Fever's broke,

70

Dave. I reckon you're going to make it. Hurtin' much?"

"Enough that it has my undivided attention." Willoughby's voice seemed to be gaining strength. "Where are we?"

"Fredericksburg. Helen Richter's place." Brubs dropped his hand away. "She was listenin' to that guardian angel of ours, I reckon. Done us a right good turn, puttin' us up till you get back on your feet." He forced a frown. "Dave, son, you had me frettin' just a tad there for a spell. Never saw a man laid out so puny over one little old lead slug."

Willoughby grimaced at a sudden twinge of pain. "It doesn't feel so little from my point of view. Who ripped my whole side off?"

"Cranky old German sawbones of a doctor." He turned as the door creaked open behind him.

Helen Richter strode to Willoughby's side, her face brightening as she stared into his eyes. "I thought I heard voices in here," she said.

"His fever's broke, ma'am," Brubs said. "I reckon that's good news."

"It surely is, Mr. McCallan." She put a hand on Willoughby's cheek, then laid her fingers against his neck and grunted in satisfaction. She cut a quick glance at Brubs. "I'll take over now. You get some rest."

"I ain't tired, ma'am."

"Do not argue with me, Mr. McCallan. You have been sitting in that chair for two days and two nights, clucking over this young man. You get some real sleep, or I will have two patients on my hands."

Willoughby raised an eyebrow at Brubs. "You've been sitting there all this time?"

Brubs felt his face color. "Now, don't you go makin' out like I'm your old maid aunt or somethin', Dave. They wasn't nothin' else to do nohow."

Helen Richter pulled the sheet down past Willoughby's waist and peered for a moment at the bandage. "You're still bleeding a bit, Mr. Willoughby. We'll get that bandage changed and then see if we can get some soup into you."

Willoughby winced as the widow loosened the knot that held the bandage in place, then forced a weak smile at Brubs. "Funny thing," he said. "I went through the whole war and never got a scratch."

Brubs said, "You always said us Johnny Rebs couldn't shoot for squat." He leaned forward to study the angry red flesh that came into view as the widow pulled the bandage away. "Don't you worry none. That ain't much worse than a little chigger bite, partner. You'll be back good as new in no time. Why, you can wear that little bitty scar like a real genuine Texan badge."

Willoughby's brow furrowed. "I suppose you have your own collection of genuine Texan badges?"

Brubs chuckled and shook his head. "Nope. Nary a bullet hole in Brubs McCallan's hide, you don't count a couple little nicks. You Yanks couldn't shoot straight, neither."

Helen Richter glared at Brubs. "Enough of your talk, Mr. McCallan." She dipped a washcloth in a pan of water on a stand by the bed. "Be gone with you. Get yourself some sleep. I will tend to your friend."

Brubs leaned against the end of the counter in Fredericksburg's general mercantile and waited patiently as the elderly clerk shuffled about, filling his order.

The stocky Texan stared wistfully through the big plateglass window at the saloon across the street. But this time he would have to leave town thirsty. Getting Willoughby patched up, keeping the two of them fed for three weeks, and replenishing their trail supplies had just about wiped out their cash. Now that the German doc had said Willoughby was well enough to ride, Brubs could admit he was getting bored with Fredericksburg. He got antsy in a hurry in a town when he was stuck without any fun money.

The clerk plopped a sack of flour onto the counter with a grunt, then picked up a pencil. "Let's see, now — coffee, flour, beans, half a side of bacon, dried apples, sulphur matches, box of .44-40 cartridges, one box Henry rimfires, two boxes .45 Colt. Comes to nine dollars and eighteen cents, mister."

Brubs cast a final longing glance at the saloon across the street, sighed, and was about to pull the small leather coin pouch from his pocket when a trio of horsemen moving into view caught his eye. The man in front was medium height, maybe five ten, but thick in the shoulders. A shock of black hair tumbled from beneath a light gray derby tugged down on his head. He carried a brace of revolvers in saddle scabbards, a third pistol in a holster high at his belt, and a carbine holstered beneath his right leg, butt pointing backward. Sunlight glinted from a spot of metal on his vest. He rode a line-backed dun gelding with a deep chest, powerful hindquarters, black mane and tail, and black stockinged feet — a horseman's mount, if Brubs had ever seen one.

The two men trailing behind seemed cast from a similar mold, young, hard-eyed and tough, one stocky and dark as an Indian, the other tall, blond, and fair-skinned. Both of them carried about the same amount of lethal hardware as the man on the dun. Brubs stabbed a thumb toward the trio and glanced at the store clerk. "Haven't seen those three around lately," he said casually. "Ornery looking bunch. Know who they are?"

The clerk bobbed his head. "Yes, sir. Texas Rangers, all three of 'em. Man in front's Sergeant Tobin Jamison. Don't know the others by name, but if they ride with Jamison you can bet they aren't wearing frilly drawers."

Brubs pursed his lips in a silent whistle. "Jamison. I've heard of that Ranger. Expected him to be nine feet tall and wearin' horns. Picks his teeth with a live rattler's fangs and can track one little snowflake through a Montana blizzard, they say.

Wonder what brings them boys up this way?"

The clerk shrugged. "Most likely after horse thieves."

The hairs on Brubs's neck prickled. "Horse thieves?"

"Yes, sir. Lots of folks around here have been losing stock. Some of the ranchers got together and asked the governor to send a good Ranger. Looks like they sent the best." He tapped stubby fingers on the counter. "Anything else for you today?"

Brubs shook his head. "Reckon not." He fished his last gold eagle from the coin pouch, handed it to the clerk, and started stowing the supplies in the possibles sack. "Any idea who Jamison's after?"

"Nope. Anybody with a craving for another man's horses, I'd guess." The clerk counted the change from the ten into Brubs's outstretched palm. "I sure wouldn't want to be a horse thief with that man on my trail."

"Me, neither, mister," Brubs said. "Me, neither." He strode through the door to the hitch rail outside, tied the possibles sack to the saddle, and swung aboard Squirrel. The idea of going home to LaQuesta was sounding a whole bunch better all of a sudden.

FIVE

Dave Willoughby dismounted gingerly, still favoring the raw scar tissue that puckered over the hole low on his left side. The pain had stopped days ago, except for the twinges he felt when the scar tissue stretched. Another week or so, he figured, and he would be as good as ever. However good that might be.

He squatted to study the tracks in the sand on the banks of the spring-fed creek that trickled toward LaQuesta, population twelve, a couple of miles to the south. The paw prints were almost as big as his hand, and they were fresh. The prints told him that the rogue mountain lion had paused here to drink, probably just after dawn. Willoughby heard the flutter of nostrils as the big roan gelding called Choctaw snorted, head erect and testing the wind. Stump Hankins had said the roan could smell an Indian or a mountain lion — a "painter," Stump called them — from a mile off. The big cat probably was still somewhere in the valley, maybe even watching from one of the juniper-studded mountains that flanked the Texas Horsetrading Company holdings.

Willoughby let his gaze drift across the valley. He saw no sign of the cat. The land itself still impressed him as much as it had the first time he had seen it almost a year ago, when he and

Brubs had brought Stump home to his eternal rest beside his wife and only son in the small grave plot behind the house a half mile away.

The lush grass was an almost obscene green against the backdrop of jagged, dry, adobe-colored mountains that flanked the valley to the east and west. The grass stayed green from early spring until first frost, testament to the water table that lay only a couple of feet beneath the valley floor. The gurgle of gently flowing water along the creek blended into a soothing melody with the rustle of cottonwood leaves in the light southwest wind. A red-tailed hawk's shrill hunting cry sounded high overhead. The hawk's call triggered a *chiing* of alarm from the covey of blue quail that lived in the tangle of berry vines a few yards up the creek.

Willoughby spotted a flash of movement on the face of a craggy mountain to the east, but relaxed as the distant form took shape. A trio of mule deer, two does and a buck with the biggest rack of antlers Willoughby had ever seen, eased down from the cover of the mountain and nuzzled the grass of the valley floor.

Choctaw snorted again, then dropped his muzzle and began cropping the grass beside the creek. That told Willoughby that the roan had caught no further scent of the mountain lion. Willoughby sighed in relief. He hadn't really wanted to find the big cat. The hunt was just an excuse to get outside, away from the confines of the small adobe house, and to test his staying power in the saddle. The mountain lion wasn't a threat to the Texas Horsetrading Company at the moment, and Willoughby took no pleasure in killing for sport. The time might come when the cat would have to be eliminated, but not today. There were no foals or calves in the valley. The ranch wasn't big enough to support a breeding herd of either horses or cattle, but it had sufficient grass and water to accommodate a fair-sized remuda for brief periods of time. As Brubs had said, it was the perfect place for the needs of a couple of honest horse thieves — far from civilization, even farther from the nearest lawman, but close enough to the Rio Grande that horses could be gathered on either side, trailed across the Rio, and sold to either Mexican or Texan buyers.

Willoughby idly wondered if Stump Hankins would approve of the way they were using his legacy, willed to the two greenhorns before the old *mesteñero* died under the guns of Gilberto Delgado's men on Mustang Mesa. He decided the old mossback of a mustanger wouldn't care as long as he and Brubs tended the graves on the mountain slope behind the house.

Willoughby stood and breathed deep of the mild air that still bore the hint of the cool remnants of the night. Mid-morning was his favorite time of day. Later, the wind would pick up, swirling heat and dust from the Mexican desert beyond the Rio Grande into the valley.

He pulled Choctaw's muzzle from the grass,

swung into the saddle, and reined the roan toward home. Willoughby's lips lifted in a slight smile. Brubs McCallan, he decided, was as full of surprises as he was full of flat-out orneriness. The bowlegged little Texan normally avoided any type of work that couldn't be done from horseback as if it was the sole cause of the plague. But on the way back from Fredericksburg, Brubs had handled all the camp cooking and cleaning chores, cared for the horses, even changed Willoughby's bandage for him, clucking and scratching about like an old mother hen. Back in LaQuesta, Brubs had even lowered his standards far enough to actually pick up a broom and sweep the place out — once — while Willoughby recuperated. The sight of Brubs McCallan with a broom in his hand had been, Willoughby mused, the ninth wonder of the world.

Willoughby pulled Choctaw to a halt between the barn and the three-room house. The walls of the house showed fresh patches where he and Brubs had replaced adobe crumbled by wind and weather. The house was little more than a cabin, but it was warm in winter and cool in summer. The whole house would have fit into the servants' quarters at the Willoughby family mansion back East, but to Dave the little adobe was the home the mansion had never been. The sprawling Colonial-style house overlooking the Ohio River was little more than a bad memory to Willoughby. Sticks, stones, thorns and all, he had come to realize, he wouldn't trade the vast expanse of sky and canyons and mountains of the Texas Big Bend country for all the money and luxury of Cincinnati. There was something about this land that grabbed a man and wouldn't let go.

He casually wondered what his family would think of him now, a common horse thief with a gunshot wound and a price — albeit an insultingly low one — on his head. A wry smile touched his lips. If they mentioned him at all, he figured, it was as the black sheep of the family. Willoughby liked the sound of that title. He felt no remorse about leaving home without a backward glance. Out here, a man was judged for what he was, not how much money he had or how big his house was. And out here, his father and brother didn't run Dave Willoughby's life. Dave did. He considered it a better than fair trade.

He kneed Choctaw to the corral gate, led the roan into the barn, and stripped the saddle. The effort brought a fresh twinge to his side and a grimace to his lips, but it took less effort and pain to handle the heavy Mexican-style saddle with each passing day. He patted Choctaw's neck a couple of times, stowed the tack, dribbled a handful of grain into a trough, and tugged absently at the leggy roan's mane as the horse ate.

Even the horses were different in the West, Willoughby mused; ugly by Eastern standards, but tough, competent, sometimes ornery, and often full of buck. He wouldn't trade Choctaw for a stable full of Eastern-bred horses with high price tags and nothing between their ears.

Willoughby left Choctaw to lip the remaining kernels of grain from the trough and made his way toward the house. He paused for a moment to study the sign between house and barn that proclaimed this to be the headquarters of the Texas Horsetrading Co. The words were painted inside the outline of an inverted horseshoe, the brand Stump had willed to Willoughby and Brubs along with the house and land. Smaller letters in the center identified the owners: *B. McCallan & D. Willoughby, Props.* The sign was showing a bit of weathering; Willoughby made himself a note to touch it up soon. He would never let Brubs know it, but Willoughby felt a sort of comfortable glow every time he looked at that sign. It was the first thing he had ever felt he owned in his life. It didn't matter that the Texas Horsetrading Company was usually flat broke. It was still half his.

Willoughby strode on to the house, pushed the door open, and came to an abrupt stop, his jaw dropping in surprise.

Brubs McCallan was taking a bath.

And nobody was even holding a gun on him.

Brubs paused in the midst of lathering his armpits with a sliver of homemade soap, bony, bowed-out knees almost touching his chest as he sat in the washtub. He still had his hat on.

"I'll be damned," Willoughby said. "I didn't know it was September yet."

Brubs puffed a bit of lather from the corner of his mustache and snorted in disgust. "Man can't

81

even take a bath without somebody insults him. Shut the door, please."

Willoughby eased the door closed, then poured himself a cup of coffee. It was rank enough to float a horseshoe. He carried the cup to the small, scarred table and sat down. "What's the occasion?"

"The occasion," Brubs said, "is that for damn nigh on to a month I been behavin' sweeter'n some Aunt Mary organizin' a Baptist camp meetin'." He reached for a brush normally used to groom horses and scrubbed his toes. "Tonight I'm makin' up for lost time. I ain't had me a drink or a woman since Goliad, and that's just flat unnatural behavior. So you and me are goin' to Symms's place, grab us a bottle, and say our howdys to Kat tonight."

Willoughby frowned. "Brubs, we don't have that much money —"

"Money. I swan, Dave Willoughby, you nag a man enough he sure as hell don't need no wife around. Toss me your razor."

"Razor? You're actually going to shave?" Willoughby rolled his eyes toward the ceiling. "Now I *know* we're in trouble." He stood, strode to the mantel, and handed the straight razor to Brubs. "Just exactly how do you propose to pay for this little party? We are broke, in case you have forgotten that little item."

Brubs flicked the straight razor open and scratched it across his jaw. "We got enough. Bottle don't cost but a couple bucks." He winced and dabbed a finger at a razor cut on his cheek. Brubs hadn't had much practice with razors.

"And Kat? She charges five dollars, if memory serves me correctly."

Brubs flashed a wide gun. "And worth ever' damn penny of it, too. Lot of woman there, amigo. Don't you fret about it. We'll get somethin' worked out — besides them kinks in your back. Way I see it, you can ride Kat proper, you can sure as hell fork a gentle horse."

Willoughby felt the color rise in his cheeks. "Brubs, Kat may be a whore, but there's no reason to talk about her like that. Anyway, I can't let you spend the last of our money on liquor and women. There are things we need worse."

Brubs said, "Speak for yourself, partner. I done got my necessaries figured out. We got plenty of grub for a couple weeks. And if you're fixin' to give yourself the vapors over money again, we're gonna get more."

"I suppose you have that worked out, too?"

"Damn straight, amigo. While you was lyin' around snoozin' the days out and growin' skin over that little cat scratch on your hide, I been workin'. Found us a market for thirty head down in Sonora. Twenty dollars apiece, more for good cow ponies."

"Where do we get these horses?"

Brubs shrugged. "We'll find 'em somewheres. We're smack-dab in the middle of hoss country. You just leave that up to me."

Willoughby sighed. "Somehow, I was afraid

you would say that."

Brubs swished the razor in the bathwater, wiped the blade on a faded towel, and tossed it to Willoughby. "You want to use this here water before I throw her out?"

Willoughby winced and shook his head. "I'll get my own. That bathwater's probably thicker than this coffee."

Dave Willoughby reined Choctaw alongside Brubs's sorrel as the two turned onto what would have been the main street of LaQuesta if the town had had streets.

LaQuesta was a haphazard scattering of adobe buildings, most of them in various states of decay. At one time LaQuesta may have been the belle of the ball in the Big Bend country, but now she was an aging and doddery dowager living out her years in poverty and neglect. Her romance with the freight wagons and stage lines that plied the California Trail waned with the end of the Gold Rush and finally faded when the freight roads moved to smoother terrain up north.

Brubs sniffed the wind and grinned. "Partner, that there is the best perfume I have smelt in many a moon."

"I don't smell anything but dust and privvies."

Brubs sighed in mock despair. "And I thought you was on your way to makin' a Texan after all," he said. "Real, genuine Texan can smell a saloon a mile off, like a coyote sniffin' up a crippled rabbit." He reined Squirrel to a stop before the only two-story building in LaQuesta. "Sawdust, tobacco smoke, stale beer, and woman. Nose music to a man dyin' from neglectin' his habits, partner."

Willoughby draped the roams reins around the sagging hitch rail and stood for a moment staring at the crude hand-lettering painted on the wall above the door. It read, SYMMS' DRY GODDS AND SALON. Barley Symms wasn't much of a speller, but he had the only store and cantina for fifty miles around. He could spell it any way he wanted.

Brubs banged the door open and strode to the crude plank bar in the dingy interior, Willoughby a step behind. Barley Symms sat behind the bar, sweat gleaming from his bald head in the weak light filtering in from a west window. Symms glanced up, scowling at the intrusion. Willoughby could tell at a glance the potbellied store owner with more hair sticking from his ears than on top of his head was in his usual condition — drunk.

"Hey, Barley," Brubs said by way of greeting. "You got any of that sheep-dip you call whiskey left?"

Symms blinked watery eyes. "Got any money?"

Brubs slapped a palm against the bar. "That old yeller hound out there got fleas? Let's have a jug over here. I'm so thirsty I ain't spit in a month."

"Two fifty."

"Two fifty!" Brubs's face colored in outrage. "You damned old bandit, it was two bucks last time!"

"And the last time you boys were in here, I wound up short two quarts. Not to mention the breakage."

"Symms, you know damn well that wasn't our fault. That drifter started the whole thing." Brubs snorted in disgust. "Insulted us somethin' fierce, sayin' old Squirrel was ugly. Man don't stand for no saddle bum bad-mouthin' a good horse. Ain't my fault Willoughby here whupped up on him."

Symms leveled a bleary stare at Brubs. "Busted my back bar mirror."

Brubs squinted at the stained, unwashed four-by-eight panel. Small cracks spread like a spider-web from a chink in one corner. "Ain't Dave's fault that cowboy had such a hard head."

"Brubs," Willoughby interrupted, "I hate to butt in on a private conversation, but I wasn't the one who threw that man over the bar."

Brubs glanced at him. "You would of if I hadn't. That's how come we're partners." He shook his head in disgust. "Two fifty for a bottle. Plumb outrageous, holdin' up a payin' customer that way."

Symms downed a swallow from the bottle in front of him and weaved on his stool. "It's my place. You don't like the price —"

Brubs lifted a hand. "I know, I know. It ain't but fifty miles to the next whiskey." He sighed. "Okay, serve it up, Symms."

"Lemma see your money."

Brubs's lower lip drooped in a wounded pout. "Symms you are the most suspiciousest soul I ever met. Ain't you ever heard of trustin' your fellow man?"

"Not where you're concerned, McCallan. Cash on the table."

Brubs reached into a pocket and dropped a five-dollar gold piece on the rough pine. "Fork over that cowboy canteen, you old coot. And a extra glass for my amigo here."

Willoughby shook his head. "No whiskey for me. I'll just have beer." Symms served the worst whiskey in the West, but the homemade brew was more than passable — and Willoughby still wasn't sure his gut was ready for hard liquor again after the abuse he had put it through in Goliad.

"Beer's fifteen cents."

Brubs slammed an open palm against the bar. "I done give you five dollars, dammit! Now, get them drinks out here or I'm gonna get mad!"

Symms shrugged, pocketed the gold piece, and reached under the bar. He thumped a bottle in front of Brubs, added a smudged shot glass, and reached for a mug. He stumbled and almost fell on his way to the beer keg a couple of steps away.

Brubs downed a shot, gasped, and grimaced. "Downright most god-awful rotgut whiskey I ever drunk, Symms." He licked his lips and grinned. "Sure does hit the spot." He poured another shot.

Symms wavered on his feet as he put Willoughby's beer in front of him, shuffled back to his perch on the stool behind the bar, and hoisted

87

his own bottle again. Another few minutes, Willoughby thought, and Symms would be passed out behind the bar again. The man drank more than he sold. It showed in the red-streaked, prominent nose and the bloodshot eyes that never quite seemed to focus.

"Where's Kat?"

"Upstairs." Symms picked up a broom, thumped the end of the handle against the ceiling, and roared, "Get your fat butt down here, woman! You got customers!"

Willoughby sipped at his beer and cocked an eyebrow at Brubs. McCallan had already lowered the level of whiskey in the bottle by three fingers and was pouring himself another. Willoughby checked the urge to tell his friend to take it easy. He owed him that much.

Symms seemed determined to match Brubs shot for shot. Willoughby watched the unspoken duel with growing interest as he nursed his beer. With the head start Symms had, Brubs was a lock to win that drinking bout.

Brubs glanced up and pursed his lips in a silent whistle. "That gal sure knows how to come through a gate."

Willoughby turned toward the staircase. Brubs was right. Kat Symms stood on the second step from the top, an ample hip cocked against the railing, blond hair brushing her shoulders. She wore a faded print housedress which buttoned down the front, though half the buttons weren't being used. Kat ran a bit to the chunky side, but the chunks were, as Brubs had often said, all in the right places.

Willoughby instinctively removed his hat. Kat smiled at him, blue eyes twinkling. "Hello, boys." Her voice was throaty and musical. "Haven't seen you in a while." She came down the stairs, hips swaying with each step.

"I reckon," Brubs said to Barley Symms, "you done raised the price on your woman, too."

Willoughby felt his face flush. He didn't know if he was embarrassed because Kat was a woman, because she was a whore, because it just didn't seem right for Brubs to be talking about her like she was a piece of meat on a butcher block, or if it was because Kat was Barley Symms's wife. Willoughby still had trouble accepting that. Maybe Symms didn't "use" her anymore, as he had said, but it still didn't seem right. Even if Kat didn't mind.

"Nope. Price's still" — Symms's words were starting to slur badly — "five bucks. Pay — in advance."

Kat strode up to Willoughby's side, propped an elbow on the bar, and smiled. "How have you been, Dave?"

Willoughby swallowed and nodded. "Fine. You?"

"Lonely," Kat said. She leaned against Willoughby. He was painfully aware of her scent of lilac water and woman and the warmth from the breast against his arm. "It's good to see you again."

89

"Hey," Brubs squawked, "how about me?"

Kat inclined her head. "It's good to see you again, too, Brubs. It's been a long time."

"We been busy, Kat. Dave here managed to get hisself shot —"

Alarm flared in Kat's blue eyes. She put a hand over Willoughby's. "Oh, that's terrible! Was it bad? Are you still in pain?"

Willoughby felt the quickening thump of his heart against his rib cage. He shook his head. "It was nothing serious. I had a good nurse."

"He sure 'nuff did. I took care of that boy nigh on to a month," Brubs said.

"I was speaking of Helen Richter," Willoughby said. "But now that you mention it, did I ever say thanks for your help?"

Brubs shrugged. "No need."

Willoughby heard a solid thump. Barley Symms's bar stool was empty. Brubs leaned over the bar, peered at the floor, and chuckled aloud. "Old Barley's done bit the dust. Out cold."

Kat's hand closed tighter over Dave's. "He'll be out for the rest of the night." Her voice was low and breathy. "Why don't we go upstairs, Dave?"

Willoughby swallowed hard. "Kat, I — we — don't have any money."

She leaned closer, her breath warm against Willoughby's neck. "That doesn't matter. No charge to you." She flashed a deliciously wicked grin. "My treat, you might say."

"Hey! How about me?"

Kat glanced at Brubs. "Your credit's good with me Brubs. You come up after I'm through with Dave."

"Now there," Brubs said, pausing to down a shot of whiskey, "is a woman after my own heart. Or something else." He refilled his glass and lifted it in a toast. "You kids have fun."

He knocked back another shot and watched as Kat led Dave up the stairs. "There just ain't no explainin' some women's druthers," he muttered. "Don't know what these females see in old Willoughby, passin' up a real Texan for that skinny Yankee. I do all the sweet talkin' and he always gets the prime filly in the cavvy. Sure wish I knowed how he done it."

Brubs leaned over the bar, plucked a bottle from beneath the pine, and glared for a moment at the unconscious Barley Symms. Spit bubbles frothed at the corner of Symms's mouth between snores. "Two fifty a jug. You damned old thief. Might as well stick a gun in a man's ear and take his last dime." He glanced toward the stairs and shrugged. "Reckon I got time to do some serious drinkin'," he said to himself. "Looks like it might be a spell before it's my turn upstairs."

Brubs McCallan was a happy man.

He was still weak in the knees — Kat Symms was mighty good at her trade — and just drunk enough to be what he would call "sociable friendly."

Kat perched on Barley Symms's stool behind

the bar, where she had taken over after the three of them had dragged her husband out of the way. She was sipping whiskey from a water glass and keeping Willoughby's beer mug filled. The pale glow of a single lantern painted highlights in her blond hair, now darkened by sweat and slightly disheveled.

Brubs had just pulled the cork from the second whiskey bottle; a third jug, purloined from beneath the back bar while Kat and Willoughby were upstairs, nestled in Brubs's saddlebags outside. He chuckled aloud. Old Barley was getting paid back for his holdup man's prices.

Kat Symms lifted a quizzical eyebrow at him. "What's so amusing, Brubs? You are grinning like a possum in a tree full of ripe persimmons."

"Just thinkin', Kat. This here is what friends is all about. Just one big happy family. I ain't had such a good time since old man Turner caught his drawers on fire up on the Colorado —"

The slam of the saloon door broke off Brubs's reverie. He turned on his stool.

The man standing in the doorway was as big as an outhouse and as ugly as a wet badger. His broad, dark face was drawn into a deep frown around a nose that had been smashed almost flat. The belt around his waist held a holstered .45 Colt, a knife big enough to use for a breaking plow, and he had a second handgun tucked beneath his waistband. He carried a Sharps Big Fifty rifle in his left hand. The ticking of the mantel clock behind the bar was loud in the sudden silence of the saloon.

"I'm a-lookin'," the big man said in a voice that threatened to flake adobe from the walls, "for a sawed-off little ex-Rebel hoss thief named McCallan."

SIX

Dave Willoughby's gut tightened as he stared at the big man in the doorway. He dropped his hand to his hip and felt his heart skid when his palm touched nothing but cloth. He had left the pistol belt and Colt upstairs at the foot of Kat's bed. Last chapter in Dave Willoughby's life, he thought, shot down in a bar because he'd left his gun beside a whore's bed. It wasn't the ending he'd had in mind.

Willoughby cut a quick glance at Brubs. The stocky Texan leaned his back against the bar, elbows resting on the rough pine, outwardly relaxed and unconcerned. "I'm McCallan, you big, ugly son of a mangy flea-bit she dog."

"Brubs —" Willoughby's warning came out hoarse and creaky.

Brubs waved a casual hand at Willoughby. "Stand easy, partner. I can handle this louse-bit excuse of a saddle tramp and never break a sweat."

The big man glared hard at Brubs in the sudden quiet. "You miserable runt, I been huntin' you nigh on to two weeks now. Fill your hand, you sorry bastard!"

Brubs shrugged. "Don't mind if I do." He reached out with his left hand, never taking his gaze from the big man's face, and picked up the whiskey bottle. "My hand's full, mister. I

94

reckon it's your move."

Willoughby glanced back at Brubs and almost swallowed his tongue. The damn fool was actually grinning.

The big man glared hard at Brubs for a few heartbeats, then propped the Sharps against the wall. He strode toward Brubs, light on his feet for such a big man. Willoughby tensed, poised to tackle him — and his jaw dropped in surprise.

The big man grabbed Brubs in a bear hug and lifted him from his feet; Brubs slapped him on the back and raised a sizable cloud of trail dust.

"How the hell have you been, you little son of a bitch?" The dark scowl was gone from the man's face. In its place was a grinning smear of tobacco-stained teeth.

"Better'n a hot buttered biscuit," Brubs said. "I figured you'd have been hung or shot by now. God, it's mighty fine to see you. Want to put me down before you bust a rib or after?" The big man lowered Brubs to the sawdust floor. Brubs turned to Dave. "Dave, this here's Archibald Thibadeau Tilghman. Everybody calls him Tige. Best damn scout in the whole Confederate army and a fair enough horse thief in his own right. Dave Willoughby, my partner."

Willoughby hesitated, still a bit stunned, then offered a hand. Tilghman's grip was like a blacksmith's vise. Willoughby wondered if the hand would still work when and if he got it back. "Pleased to meet you, Mr. Tilghman."

"Call me Tige. I done forgot my real name till

that no-account saddle bum here throwed her back at me. Good to meet you, Willoughby. Anybody with enough rawhide to ride with Brubs McCallan's all right in my book." He finally released Willoughby's hand.

"Tige, this pretty thing here's Katherine Symms," Brubs said. "Goes by the name of Kat."

Tilghman swept the sweat-stained hat from his head and bowed slightly. "Pleasure to meet you, ma'am. Excuse my language back there. I kinda got excited, findin' this whelp after ridin' all over this god-awful country. No offense intended."

Kat smiled and nodded. "None taken, Mr. Tilghman. Welcome to LaQuesta."

"Kat, hand us another glass. Looks like old Tige needs a nip of honey."

"Reckon I got time for a quick snort or two, at that," Tilghman said.

"You in a hurry or somethin'?"

Tilghman shrugged. "Hopin' to make it to Mexico by sunup tomorrow." He lifted the shot glass, sniffed the liquor, downed the whiskey in one swallow, and grimaced. "Lord have mercy. That's the worst rotgut I ever had."

"It's on the house," Kat said.

Tilghman licked his lips and held out his glass. "In that case, it's the nectar on the reddest rose. Fill her up again, ma'am."

"What are you on the run for this time, Tige?" Brubs said.

"Nothin' much to fret about. Spot of woman

trouble over in Little Rock."

Brubs downed his own drink and grinned at the big man. "You never done nothin' little in your miserable misspent life, Tige. Woman trouble, eh? Who'd you kill this time?"

Tilghman's brow wrinkled. "My brother-in-law. Damn me if I can figure how come the law got so riled up about it. Wasn't nothin' but a family matter. Reckon we got too damn civilized up in Arkansas." The frown faded. "Anyhow, he ain't gonna be hittin' my sister no more. Fair trade. I was lookin' to move on anyhow. Arkansas's gettin' so crowded since the war a man can't swing a cat without somebody gets scratched. People all over the place. Won't give a man room to breathe."

Brubs sighed. "Ain't that a sure 'nuff fact. Country's plumb et up with civilization. You won't have that trouble in LaQuesta, you want to stay a spell."

"Noticed that. I like to have never found this damn place. Nobody seems sure where it's at."

"Not unless they was born here." Brubs held the bottle up to the lantern light, measuring the level. "It ain't that I ain't glad to see you just for the hell of it and old time's sake, Tige, but you got my curious stirrin'. Somethin' special bring you down here?"

Tilghman downed the whiskey and sighed. "Yep. Figured you boys might be lookin' for some cheap hosses. Real cheap." Tilghman lifted an eyebrow in Willoughby's direction. "Heared you had some trouble. How's the bullet hole, son?"

"Mending well, thank you."

"You talk funny, Willoughby. When you talk at all. Which, I notice, ain't much."

"I suppose I'm out of practice. It's hard to get a word in edgewise when you ride with Brubs McCallan."

Brubs snorted. "Hell, there ain't much talk in old Dave worth diggin' out, anyway. College boy. Got no horse stories, women yarns, or barroom brawl tales in him, and he sure don't talk much about the war. He was Yankee, but don't hold it agin' him, Tige."

Tilghman raised the other eyebrow. "What outfit?"

"First Ohio Volunteers. Artillery."

Tilghman hoisted his glass. "Pretty fair outfit, the First Ohio." He downed the drink and wiped a big hand over his mouth. "Doubt we ever shot at each other. Brubs and me was with Hood. Why, I remember one time, up someplace in Virginia, we was —"

"Tige," Brubs interrupted, "I just heard what you said a minute ago. Hold off on them war stories. Somethin' about real cheap horses?"

"Oh. Yeah. That's why I come lookin' for you two in the first place." He tapped thick fingertips on the pine bar. "Buried a friend of mine up Seguin way a spell back, week or ten days ago. Me and him shared some time in a Yank prison camp. Anyhow, this friend done lost his horse

98

ranch, lock, stock, and haystack." Tilghman shook his head in dismay. "Rich San Antonio banker and one of the nickel-squeezer's business buddies, man name of Pettibone, called in a loan —"

Brubs slammed a palm onto the bar. "Petti-bone! Lawrence T. Pettibone?"

"The same. Owner of the Bexar and Rio Grande freight line. You know him?"

"I should whisper to shout we know the damned old tightwad." Brubs snorted in disgust. "Twenty-five dollars. I never been so insulted in all my born days."

"Twenty-five dollars?" Tilghman looked confused.

"That is the reward Pettibone put on our heads," Willoughby explained. "We were working as guards on a freight shipment. We rode into an ambush and lost the wagons. Pettibone blamed us for it."

A slow grin replaced the frown on Tilghman's face. "Damn me if you boys ain't gettin' plumb notorious. A whole twenty-five dollars."

"Get back to the horses," Brubs prompted.

Tilghman said, "This banker and Pettibone took the place over when Frank couldn't pay."

"I'm sorry to hear about your friend's misfortune, Tige," Willoughby said.

"That ain't the worst of it. Frank Merrell had worked his whole life since the war buildin' that Bar F outfit. After they told him he had two days to clear out, he went out in the barn, stuck a

99

pistol in his mouth, and pulled the trigger." Tilghman sighed heavily. "Never expected ol' Frank to do somethin' like that, not after what he'd been through. The Yanks couldn't kill him, but them money grubbers did, sure enough."

"Tige, you're ridin' off the trail again. The horses?"

Tilghman turned back to Brubs. "I'm gettin' to that. Frank had nigh on to forty head. Mostly brood mares and cow horses. Was crossin' Kentucky and Tennessee racin' stock studs on some good Texas-bred mares." He drained his glass and waited until Kat refilled it. "Got some better'n fair cow ponies out of that cross. The hosses is still on Frank's place three miles northwest of Seguin. Nobody watchin' over 'em but a bank clerk who can't see ten feet without his specs. I thought maybe you boys'd find that interestin'."

Brubs leaned across the bar and liberated another bottle. "That's a sure 'nuff fact. Mighty interestin'. Special interestin' if Pettibone's got a hand in it." He uncorked the bottle. "How'd you find out where we was, Tige?"

"Aunt Helen. Over by Fredericksburg."

"Helen Richter? Didn't know she was your aunt."

"She ain't by blood," Tilghman said. "Sort of a step-neighbor-in-law to a cousin twice removed on my pa's side, near as I can figure." He shrugged. "Anyhow, I dropped in on Aunt Helen for supper about a week ahead of this deputy marshal from Little Rock. Aunt Helen and me got to talkin'. She told me about how you boys done her a good turn, that you owned an outfit called the Texas Horsetradin' Company in LaQuesta." Tilghman added, "So I come lookin'."

Brubs refilled Tilghman's glass. "I'm happier'n a skunk in a henhouse you found us, Tige. Just so happens I got a buyer down in Mexico lookin' for some good cow ponies. Been wonderin' where we'd get 'em. How's about throwin' in with us?"

Tilghman shook his head. "I ain't stole no horses since the war. Besides, that star-packer from Little Rock most likely ain't far behind me. I'd as soon not kill him if I don't have to, so I reckon I'll drift on over the Rio." Tilghman turned to Willoughby. "Brubs ever tell you about the time we swiped that Yank general's pet horse?"

Willoughby shook his head. "Brubs doesn't talk much about the war, either."

Tilghman tossed back his drink and chuckled. "Stole that horse damn near from inside the general's tent. Snuck through three picket lines and the general's personal guards and led his horse off." Tilghman laughed aloud. "Sure would like to have seen the general's face next mornin'. I bet he was squawlin' and howlin' like a wet cat."

"Reckon so," Brubs said. The grin came back, but it was getting a bit crooked and his eyes didn't quite focus. Brubs was packing a fair load of Symms's Old Gutscorcher, Willoughby real-

101

ized. "That general sent a whole cavalry company out huntin' us. Hell, me and Tige coulda put the whole Yank army afoot, we'd have had the time."

Tilghman finished his drink and pushed away from the bar. "I'd best get me a move on. You two get down to Mexico City, look me up." He offered Willoughby a hand and squeezed Brubs's shoulders a final time. "Good huntin', boys." He strode through the door into the night air. The mantel clock chimed eleven.

"Now, there," Brubs said, his words slightly slurred, "is one mighty fine hombre. Pulled my bacon out of the skillet a couple times in the war. And thanks to old Tige, now we know where them horses we need's comin' from."

Willoughby drained his beer mug and waved off Kat's offer of a refill. "Brubs," he said, "it could be chancy. Pettibone might send everybody, including the cook, after us."

Brubs grinned crookedly. "Hell, partner, life's chancy anyway. Might as well have some fun along the way. And there ain't no better way to get even with old Lawrence T. Pettibone and make us some good money to boot."

Willoughby leaned against the bar and sighed heavily. *"Le continuel ouvrage de votre vie, c'est bâtir la mort."*

"Talk American, amigo. What the hell's that mean?"

"A quote from Montaigne. 'The ceaseless labor of your life is to build the house of death.' "

102

Willoughby pushed away from the bar. "Unfortunately, I think Montaigne was referring to your life's labors and my house of death. Come on, Brubs. If we're going into the lion's den, we need to get you sobered up first. I'd hate to wind up as a big cat's hair ball."

Brubs McCallan peered from the edge of a stand of pecan trees toward the ranch house and barns a hundred yards away.

Frank Merrell had built well. The house and barn were made of split logs, the corrals from peeled and seasoned poles. A black buggy waited at the front hitch rail, a chestnut gelding dozing in the harness.

Half a dozen brood mares, heavy with foals, stood in the shallow water of the stock pond behind the barn to escape the pesky heel flies. A few chickens scratched in the dirt for a final time before going to roost in the henhouse near the barn as the sun dropped toward the western horizon. It looked to be a comfortable layout, Brubs thought, one that had taken a lot of hard work to carve from the rolling, wooded hills. Too much hard work for the likes of Lawrence T. Pettibone and some starched-shirt banker to steal without working up an honest sweat. Or even a dishonest one, for that matter."

Brubs draw back into the shadows as the front door opened and a skinny man in a bowler hat and silk suit emerged, unhitched the chestnut, and swung onto the buggy seat. The off rear wheel creaked as the driver reined the horse south toward the Seguin road. He had been in the house for about two hours. Brubs figured it must have been the banker. Undertakers and bankers were about the only people in Seguin who could afford silk suits. Lawrence T. Pettibone could maybe afford it, but he'd never spend good money for a town suit. That old skinflint could squeeze a peso until the Mexican eagle looked like a sparrow stepped on by a draft horse.

Bulbs started at the sound of a twig cracking underfoot behind him. He spun, thumb on the hammer of the .44 Henry rimfire, then grunted in relief as Willoughby stepped into view from behind the bole of a big tree.

"Your friend Tilghman was right, Brubs," Dave said softly. "There are twenty or so good geldings in the west pasture." He nodded toward the house. "Did our man leave?"

"Just now rode off. I reckon that means there ain't nobody home but that four-eyed clerk." He glanced at the lowering sun. "We'll give it a few more minutes, then persuade that feller to lend us them horses. Time it's light enough to read tracks, we'll be way down the trail toward Mexico."

Willoughby frowned. "Brubs, I'd hate for the clerk to get hurt. He looks like a harmless old man."

Brubs shrugged. "We ain't gonna hurt him without he does somethin' dumb, and a man gets smart quick with a Winchester stuck in his ear.

Got the packhorses ready?"

"All set."

Brubs sat down, his back against the trunk of a tree. "Might's well get comfortable, partner. It ain't time to go to work yet." He sighed. "Sure wish you wouldn't of been so feisty about us layin' over a couple hours in Seguin. I know these two gals there —"

"Is there any town in Texas," Willoughby interrupted, "where you *don't* know two girls?"

Brubs said, "Just LaQuesta, but I reckon you could count Kat as two where partners like us is concerned. Course, I ain't been to every town in Texas, but I'm workin' on it."

Willoughby squatted on his heels beside Brubs. "It is possible," he said, "that soon we will own the dubious distinction of being run out of every town in Texas. If we live so long."

Brubs picked up a couple of last fall's pecans, cracked them together in a palm, and picked out the fragments of nut meat. He chewed on the pecans for a moment in silence then said, "Sure is gonna be fun to get even with old man Pettibone. I'd like to see his face when he finds out the horses he stole in the first place got swiped back."

Willoughby glanced at the rapidly darkening sky above the pecan grove. "I didn't realize you carried a grudge so long, Brubs. After all, Pettibone *did* bail us out of the San Antonio jail."

"And he was gonna make us work off the fine at a dollar a day." Brubs spat out a bit of pecan shell. "We'd a still been workin' for the old coot if them bandits hadn't jumped us. Maybe they done us a favor. We wouldn't of had our own business by now." Brubs cocked an eyebrow at Willoughby. "Speakin' of which, I reckon it's about time to get to work. Got to put in an honest night's labor for an honest day's profit." He rose lightly to his feet. "Let's go pay us a little social call on this here bank clerk."

Brubs led the way as the two slipped on foot to the back door of the house. Lantern light glowed from a kitchen window. Brubs paused to pull his bandanna over his mouth and nose, motioned for Willoughby to do the same, then pushed gently on the door. It was barred. He knocked.

"Who is it?" The voice from inside was reedy and nervous.

"Friends of Mr. Pettibone," Brubs said cheerfully. "Got a message for you."

Footsteps shuffled slowly to the door. Brubs heard the scrape and thump as the bar dropped. The door swung open. A stooped man with spectacles as thick as windowpanes stood in the doorway. "What's the message?"

"Forty-four caliber," Brubs said. He stuck the muzzle of his rifle almost in the old man's left nostril. The clerk's face went ash-gray. "Just back in slow and easy, friend. This old Henry's got a hair trigger."

The clerk raised his hands. "I don't have any money here — it's all at — the bank."

"Ain't money we want," Brubs said. He nodded toward a straight-backed chair at the kitchen table. "Have yourself a set-down, old-timer."

"Mister, please — I got a wife and widowed daughter and grandkids."

"We ain't gonna hurt you none." Brubs's tone was sympathetic, if a bit muffled by the bandanna over his mouth. "We got to tie you up, but we'll make it as easy on you as possible. Your boss'll likely be back a little after daylight to cut you loose."

The old man sat down. Willoughby tugged a length of three-strand rope from beneath his belt. The bank clerk's fingers shook as Willoughby bound his wrists, careful not to pull the rope too tight. There was no need to make an innocent man suffer. Willoughby tied off the rope around the clerk's ankles, then stood and nodded.

Brubs puffed out the oil lamp. "No reason to chance burnin' the place down with an old man tied up in it. Come on, partner. Let's go borrow some horses."

The first faint gray of dawn smudged the eastern horizon before Brubs, riding point with the stolen horses dutifully following, reined Mouse to a stop beside the Atascosa River.

Brubs slouched in the saddle, studying the crossing. The river ran low at this time of year, little more than a meandering trickle less than hock-deep to the little gray mustang between Brubs's knees. The bend of the stream touched the west bank here, forming a shallow pool of sluggish but reasonably clear water.

Willoughby, who had been riding drag and leading the packhorses, kneed his black alongside Brubs's mount.

"This'll do, partner," Brubs said. "We'll stop here for a little spell. Let the horses water and graze a bit before we move on. I'd be a sight less antsy if we put a few more miles between us and Seguin before we hole up for a good rest."

Willoughby lifted himself in the stirrups and rubbed a hand across his saddle-numbed backside. "How far do you calculate we've come?"

Brubs squinted into the growing dawn, then shrugged. "As the crow flies, maybe thirty, thirty-five miles. Tolerable more countin' the switchbacks and false trails we laid along the San Antonio Road."

"Which brings up a question," Willoughby said. "Why are we making such an effort — and in the dark, at that — to hide our tracks? We never bothered to do that before." He leveled a questioning stare at Brubs. "I might add that I've never seen you quite this edgy before."

Brubs spat. "Partner, this country's just plumb crawlin' with horse thieves. Man's gotta be careful in these parts." He turned to study the remuda with care as the light improved, then nodded his approval. "We got us some mighty good cow ponies here, Dave. Bring top dollar down in Mexico." He stepped from the saddle. "I'll rustle up some kindlin'. You break out that coffeepot. I get plumb twitchy when I ain't had my sunup coffee."

Willoughby had just poured his second cup when Brubs abruptly raised a hand, his head cocked to one side.

"What is it?"

Brubs yanked his pistol from the holster. "Horse comin'. Movin' fast. Grab your rifle."

Willoughby heard the hoofbeats then. The horse was approaching the camp at a lope. He dropped his cup, sprinted the few feet to the black, and swept his Winchester from the scabbard. He cocked the rifle as the hoofbeats neared.

"Well, I'll be damned," Brubs said. "Look what we got here. The devil horse done come back home."

The coyote dun gelding loped into camp, the remnants of a saddle flopping beneath his belly. The bridle reins were broken off, the shanks of the bit twisted and bent. The dun slowed to a trot, then stopped and nuzzled the neck of Willoughby's black gelding.

"Looks like old Malhumorado found his sweetie again," Brubs grumbled. "Them two horses wasn't both geldings I'd sure think they was somethin' mighty funny goin' on between 'em. Nuzzlin' and snortin' like they was courtin'."

Willoughby finally shook off his surprise at the unexpected appearance of the dun. The horse was aptly named; in Spanish, *malhumorado* roughly translated as "bad tempered" and the

109

term fit. Brubs had described the animal best the first time they had seen the coyote dun in the mustang *manada* captured early in their career. "Meanest and ugliest horse I ever seen," Brubs had said. "Pigeon-toed, cow-hocked, got a rump sharper than a roadrunner's tail, dish-faced, Roman-nosed, one eye's cloudy, and he's got a head so long he'd have to rear up to eat."

Beneath the surface ugly, the coyote dun was a good horse, at least to Willoughby; he had a soft mouth, was quick to the rein, and tough enough to go two days and nights and barely break a sweat. Malhumorado had bucked Brubs off every time he had tried to ride him, but never so much as humped his back with Willoughby. Brubs had never fully recovered from that.

Willoughby stroked the horse's neck and peered at the saddle beneath the gelding's belly. The saddle was a total wreck, both stirrups torn away, the horn sheared off even with the battered pommel, and it was held in place only by the frayed front cinch.

"Wonder what poor cowboy this crazy Mexican plug killed this time?" Brubs said. He unsheathed his knife and sliced through the cinch leather. The battered saddle landed with a soft thud. The dun nuzzled Willoughby's side and tried to scratch his ears against Willoughby's chest.

Brubs walked around the animal, shaking his head in disbelief. "That fool horse has got two more brands on him now," he said. "Didn't think there was that much empty hide left to put an iron on." The dun snapped a kick toward him, barely missing his knee. Brubs squawked and ducked aside. "Still got that same even disposition," he muttered, "mad all the time."

"Brubs, just because he doesn't happen to like you personally doesn't mean he isn't a decent horse," Willoughby said. "Wonder what he's doing out here?"

Brubs shrugged. "Probably headed back to his home country on Mustang Mesa. That broomtail's been stole and sold so many times he probably knows ever' square foot of Texas and the Indian Nation to boot."

"So what do we do with him?"

Brubs turned his head and spat. "If I had any sense, I'd say shoot him before he gets one or both of us killed. But if the idiot wants to tag along, I reckon we'll let him. We can sell him again, maybe find somebody we don't special like." He glanced at the sky. "Might as well gather our truck and move on, Dave. Day's half gone and not a lick of work done. You better saddle up old Choctaw whilst I ease them horses back together."

Willoughby lifted an eyebrow. "Why Choctaw?"

"That roan's the best river horse I ever seen."

Willoughby frowned and stared at the sluggish stream. "What does that matter? It can't be more than knee-deep."

Brubs swung aboard Mouse, the creak of saddle leather loud in the still morning air. "Ain't how deep the water is that matters. This here is the Atascosa River. In Mex lingo, *atoscosa* means boggy."

"Boggy?"

"Yep. Quicksand on this little crick's worse than the Canadian or the Red." He leaned over and spat. "Seen it bad enough to bog mosquitoes. Just sucked 'em right under, and them a-flappin' and a-squawkin'. Course, they was big skeeters. Stand flat-footed and tom a turkey hen, some of 'em."

"Quicksand?"

"Don't fret it none, partner," Brubs said. "Old Choctaw'll lead these horses right across."

"Choctaw?" Willoughby's face went pale. The coffee turned into a cold lump in his stomach. "You mean you want *me* to lead the way across a river full of quicksand?"

"Nothin' to it, Dave. You just trust old Choctaw. Course if he makes a mistake and starts to bog, kick out of them stirrups and jump as far as you can. Seen a man didn't get clear of a bogged-down horse up on the Cimarron once. Hung up in a stirrup." Brubs shook his head sadly. "That horse just went to fightin' and lungin' right on top of poor old Duggie. Tore him plumb to pieces. Duggie was a stout man, too."

Willoughby glared at him for a moment. "You are truly a comfort to a man, Brubs McCallan."

Brubs said, "Reckon I always have looked on

112

the sunshine side of the rock at that, partner. Saddle up. Time's a-wastin'." He reined Mouse toward the remuda grazing along the side of the river.

Willoughby stripped the saddle, switched the pack from Choctaw to the black, and cinched his rig in place on the leggy roan. He paused to pat Choctaw's neck. The roan nudged Willoughby's shoulder, smearing grass-stain slobbers over the pale blue cloth. "Get me to the other side of this river alive," Willoughby said to the horse, "and you can blow snot right in my face if you want."

Willoughby fought back a sudden push of urgency from his bladder as he nudged Choctaw to the riverbank. The roan dropped his head, looked left and right, snorted once, and turned aside. Willoughby gave Choctaw his head. The roan trotted downstream a few yards, then stepped onto the reddish sand of the river bottom.

Willoughby's bladder twitched again as he looked down. The roan's front hoof seemed to push the sand down a good three inches; when he lifted the hoof, water seeped into the depression left by the horseshoe. Choctaw abruptly turned upstream, walked a few yards, then lifted into an easy fox-trot toward the far bank.

Willoughby breathed a sigh of relief. He twisted in the saddle to watch as the pack animals and the rest of the remuda followed Choctaw's twisting path across the river. "Looks like we're going to make it fine, Choctaw —"

Willoughby's soft comment ended in a startled yelp as the coyote dun nipped a young bay's flank. The bay bolted a couple of yards — and went belly-deep in a bog. Willoughby barked a quick curse, stripped his rope from the tie-down, and spurred Choctaw toward the panicked and floundering bay. Willoughby felt the roan's muscles quiver. Choctaw fought the reins for a moment, then gingerly sidled closer to the bogged horse. Willoughby flipped a loop over the bay's head, dallied, and turned Choctaw toward the far bank.

It was like trying to drag a rock the size of a house.

"Ease up, Dave!" Brubs yelled as he spurred Mouse toward him. "You'll choke him to death!"

Willoughby fed slack through the dally.

"Gimme the rope," Brubs said. "Take mine. Get a loop around that horse's butt."

"How —"

"Take the damn rope out there on foot and put it around his rump! Move, man! We're gonna lose him!"

Willoughby bailed out of the saddle, grabbed Brubs's lariat, and sprinted toward the bogged horse. The sucking sand grabbed at one of his boots and sent him sprawling into the gravy-like mix of mud and water. Willoughby struggled to his feet and floundered a couple of steps closer, the lariat slippery in his hand. He fought against the powerful drag of the bog, managed to toss a

114

loop over the horse's hips, and pulled the slack.

"Now!" Brubs yelled. "Throw me the rope!"

Willoughby heaved the coiled hemp toward Brubs. The effort of the throw toppled Willoughby toward the bay's shoulder just as the terrified horse lunged. The sharp bone of the bay's withers caught Willoughby under the chin. The solid whack snapped Willoughby's head back, sent his hat spinning, and fired a flash of light before his eyes. His cheek flopped into the mud.

"Get out of the way!" Willoughby heard Brubs yell over the ringing in his ears. "He's comin' out! Don't let him get on top of you!"

Willoughby looked up, blinked, and squirmed aside a split second before a flailing front hoof slapped into the watery mud where his head had been. The bay's forequarters were free of the quicksand, hauled loose by the pull of the rope around his rump. Willoughby half rolled, half swam, windmilling his arms and legs until he was a yard away from the struggling bay. The horse's hind legs cleared the bog with a sucking slurp. Moments later the bay stood on the far bank, its eyes walled, nostrils flared, and muddy sides heaving in panic.

Willoughby slithered free of the sucking mud and crawled like a salamander on his belly as he fought for firm footing. After what seemed an eternity he heaved himself onto the dry bank. He shook his head, wiped a muddy hand across his eyes and squinted up at Brubs. The stocky

Texan knelt by his side.

"You done mighty fine there, partner," Brubs said. He slapped Willoughby on the shoulder. Mud flew. "We like to have lost a thirty-dollar horse there on account of that crazy coyote dun of yours."

"A thirty-dollar *horse?*" Willoughby gasped. "What the hell about *me?*"

Brubs's said, "Why, son, I wasn't worried none about you. Seen right off you had a hold of things. Besides, good horses is hard to come by." He wiped the mud from his hand against his pants. "Reckon you're all right?"

Willoughby finally dug enough mud from one eye to manage a bleak scowl. "Hell, yes, I'm all right. I get damn near sucked into a bottomless pit of quicksand, my brains rattled by a crazy horse, and I've got enough mud on me to build a two-story adobe. I have never" — he paused to pry a wad of mud from his right ear — "been better in my whole miserable life, thank you very much."

Brubs said, "Glad to hear that, partner. Damned if you ain't a sight, though. Ain't a place on you's not plastered up like one of them mud dolls the Tonkawa squaws make for their papooses."

Willoughby dug more mud from the other ear hole. "How come *I* was the one had to go in there?"

Brubs winked. "Wasn't no use in both of us gettin' muddy, and you're the one takes a bath

116

ever' week anyhow."

"One of these days, Brubs McCallan," Willoughby grumbled, "I am going to whip your butt. Just to give myself a special treat."

"Now you're talkin', partner. Shoot, you done showed more signs of gettin' Texanized. I seen you grab your hat on the way out of that little mud puddle." Brubs stood and brushed his palms together. "Better get mounted up. It's still a long way to Mexico and we got some horses to move."

SEVEN

Dave Willoughby came awake groggy and reluctantly. The weight of forty-eight hours of hard riding with less than six hours of sleep rode heavy on his shoulders.

He cracked one eye open as something nudged into his hip. The night sky overhead was still black, illuminated only by starlight and a thin sliver of moon perched low in the western sky.

"Rise and shine, mornin' glory," Brubs said cheerfully. "Half the day's gone and we ain't hit a lick of work yet."

Willoughby groaned aloud. "What time is it?"

"Nigh on to four o'clock, close as I can tell."

"Four o'clock in the morning," Willoughby grumbled. "What the hell has you so-called genuine Texans convinced that sunrise will kill you if you're still asleep when it happens?"

Brubs said, "This here's the best part of the day, amigo. Nice and cool. Good travelin' time. No need to waste her lyin' around and snorin'. You saddle up while I fix us a bit of bacon. I'd like to be a few miles down the trail by full light."

Willoughby inverted his boot and banged his hand against the heel. Scorpions and other critters that were not especially friendly to humans had a habit of camping out in a man's boots at night in this country. "How far have we come already? It seems as if we've been pushing these

118

horses for a week."

Brubs's brow wrinkled for a moment as he pondered the question. "Near on to a couple hundred miles, give or take twenty or thirty. Few more days, we'll be across the Rio. Three, four days after that, you'll be sleepin' late as you want and wakin' up beside some cute little señorita."

Willoughby knocked a fuzzy black spider out of his second boot. The spider glared at him. Willoughby glared back. His eyelids felt like they were lined with grit. He pulled on his hat and reached for his gun belt.

Brubs had a small fire started by the time Willoughby tied his canvas groundsheet and blankets into a tight roll. Willoughby strode to the picket line, a rope tied between two mesquites, where the coyote dun and Brubs's sorrel waited. He had been riding the coyote dun for two days. It was the only way he could think of to keep the horse from causing trouble.

Willoughby saddled and bridled the two horses and paused to squint toward the meadow along the east side of the riverbank. He had always had excellent night vision, but now he could barely make out the blurred forms of the other horses. A few were grazing, the rest standing and dozing. Willoughby had a feeling Brubs wouldn't have called a halt last night if the stolen horses hadn't been as exhausted as they were.

Brubs didn't seem to feel the miles. He squatted by the fire, whistling the Confederate marching song, "The Bonnie Blue Flag" — off-key, as usual — while he sliced strips of bacon into a sputtering skillet. Brubs wasn't the world's best camp cook, but Willoughby was too tired to take over the kitchen detail. He remembered it had been called "mess" in the army. After eating Brubs's cooking a few times, Willoughby thought he understood the term a little better.

The camp on the West Nueces River was a peaceful spot, soothed by the gentle murmur of water in the streambed. A light breeze blew cool from the rocky slopes of the scrub oak-studded hills that marked the Balcones Escarpment to the north and west. The breeze whispered through the leaves of dense mesquite thickets that bracketed the campsite. A coyote yelped in the distance; at the edge of camp a pack rat crouched beneath the safety of a big prickly pear pad, its eyes reflecting demonic red points in the firelight.

Willoughby had thought he was too tired to eat, but the smell of sizzling bacon and boiling coffee triggered a rumble in his gut. The stomach was a bullheaded organ, he mused. No matter what the rest of the body felt, when the belly got empty it took charge.

Willoughby still felt grubby. He had ridden almost an entire day covered in mud and with the sand of the Atascosa River bog chafing every fold in his skin. A hurried dip in a small spring at one water hole had helped some, but Willoughby couldn't shake the feel of sand in his teeth. He wasn't sure he would ever feel completely clean again. Right now he missed only one thing about the big mansion back East — the oversized bathtub and thick cotton towels.

Well, he admitted to himself, maybe he did miss the quadroon girl who worked as the Willoughbys' upstairs maid a little bit. He wondered idly what had happened to the girl after the war, if she was freed in accord with President Lincoln's decree. Willoughby doubted it. Slaves were valuable and hired help had to be paid.

It had always struck Dave Willoughby as hypocritical that his father and brother never missed a chance to publicly rant and rave against slavery, while all the time they had owned more than a half dozen blacks. His disgust deepened when he realized the family owned a sizable chunk of several companies involved in the war effort. Powder and weapons makers, lead foundries, railroads. The familial explosion of moral indignation over the slavery issue wasn't from sympathy for the black people. It was from an intense worship of the almighty dollar. And when he saw firsthand on the battlefields the carnage his family's business holdings fed, Willoughby's split with home was final.

He had never gone back to Cincinnati after the war. He drifted west, wound up in Texas, and never even bothered to write his folks. He hadn't forgotten them. He had simply fired them. As Brubs would say, they wasn't worth their salt as family nohow.

"Chuck's near ready, partner," Brubs chirped

from the fire. "Grab your mess kit and load up. Might be a spell 'fore we get another chance at hot grub."

Willoughby rummaged in the possibles sack, found his tin plate and cup, and squared by the fire. Brubs forked several slices of overcooked bacon onto Willoughby's plate and reached for the coffeepot.

"This stuff'll put the hair back on you, partner," he said with a grin. "Seen a horsefly would have weighed half a pound buzz over the pot a minute ago. The fumes was so strong they stopped that critter dead in its tracks and tore its wings plumb off. But you talk about strong coffee — they was this time up on the Cimarron when old Cooter Devry made a pot so strong it took four men just to lift it. So thick we couldn't drink it, so we just shaved strips off it and et it like jerky —"

Willoughby said, "Just pour the coffee, Brubs." He held out his cup.

The two men ate quickly and, as far as Willoughby was concerned, in blessed silence. It seemed to him that the only time Brubs stopped talking was when he was feeding his face. But, he had to admit, the stocky Texan's yarns were sort of entertaining. They helped pass the time.

Willoughby gathered the plates and cooking utensils and turned toward the creek to wash the morning grub wreck when a quiet word from Brubs brought him up short.

"Dave, we maybe got some troubles here." He

pointed toward the horses in the meadow. Choc-taw stood stock-still, ears cocked upriver, nostrils flared as he tested the wind. The big roan snorted, tossed its head, and pawed the turf with a front hoof.

"What's got into Choctaw?"

"I got no idea," Brubs said, "but when that roan goes on point like a high-dollar huntin' dog, a man ought to get a mite cautious."

Willoughby felt the stir of concern. Brubs McCallan didn't booger at shadows. And right now, he looked a bit spooked. Brubs slipped his Colt from its holster, spun the cylinder to check the loads, and picked up his rifle.

"Could be a lobo wolf, maybe a mountain lion," he said. "Maybe somethin' or maybe nothin'. Old Stump Hankins always said that roan could smell trouble further'n a man could see it. I'm gonna take a look." Brubs went to the saddled sorrel. "Douse the fire and hustle up with that truck," he said over his shoulder. "Get ready to move them horses out quick, just in case."

Willoughby forgot his usual neatness fetish. The chuck wreckage got a quick swish in the river and went into the packs only half clean. He was in the saddle before Brubs topped the ridge, headed back to camp. He had the sorrel in a long lope. It wasn't a good sign. Brubs never hurried a horse without a reason.

He pulled Squirrel to a sliding stop at Wil-loughby's side. His face looked a touch pale, and he had the old Henry rifle in his hand.

"What is it, Brubs?"

"Injuns. About a half mile west of the ridge."

Willoughby's hand tightened on the reins. "Hunting party?"

Brubs shook his head, his expression grim. "Wearin' war paint. Comanches, near as I could tell. Probably bronco bucks jumped the reservation, lookin' to make a name for theirselves on a raid down in Mexico."

Willoughby's blood went cold. "How many?"

"Partner, there's more feathers out there than you'll find at a turkey roost an hour past sundown. I got to tell you, I ain't likin' this a whole bunch."

"Do you think they know we're here?"

Brubs shook his head. "If they did, they'd of been on my tail and we'd be short some hair and horses by now."

"What do we do?"

"We ease out quiet-like, gather them horses and push 'em into the mesquites. Then we hunker down like a boogered rabbit and wait till they go past us. There's a time for runnin' and a time for hidin'. This here's hidin' time."

The hair on Willoughby's forearms tingled. "What happens if they spot us?"

Brubs said, "You don't even want to think on that." His grin seemed forced. "Don't you fret none. Ain't nothin' gonna happen to us. We got us a guardian angel." He reined Squirrel toward the remuda scattered across the meadow. "Let's gather some horses. Don't make no more noise about it than can be helped."

Dave Willoughby had no idea how much time had passed since he and Brubs had eased the horse herd deep into the heavy mesquites, but it seemed like a lifetime. Every time a horse snorted, his gut twisted; even the beat of his own heart seemed loud enough to be heard for a mile. Sweat beaded on his forehead and trickled down to sting his eyes. He swiped at it with a shirt-sleeved forearm, winced at the creak of saddle leather the movement caused, and tightened his grip on the receiver of the Winchester in his hand. The metal was slick with sweat. Brubs sat on Squirrel only a few feet away, yet almost obscured by the thorned limbs and thin green mesquite leaves.

"Dave?" Brubs's voice was little more than a whisper.

"Yes?"

"I'm gonna sneak out on top that ridge for a look-see. Them Injuns ought to be long gone by now. If they ain't, and they spot me, don't try to win no medals. Slam the spurs to that ugly dun and light a shuck."

"I'll go look."

"No, you won't," Brubs said softly. "You was artillery. You don't know sneakin' like us foot soldiers. Set tight." Willoughby heard the creak of saddle leather and the scrape of mesquite thorns against leggings, then nothing but silence.

Brubs was gone for what seemed an eternity. Willoughby's heart leapt at a rustling in the brush; he lifted the Winchester, then quickly lowered it as Brubs rode into view.

"Ain't nobody after your hair now, amigo." Brubs's voice had a relieved, almost happy, lilt to it. "We're movin' out."

Willoughby's breath whooshed out in a deep sigh of relief. He slid the Winchester back into the scabbard and went hunting for horses.

Willoughby had to make two trips back into the thicket before all the horses were accounted for. He reined the coyote dun alongside Brubs's sorrel. "What now?"

Brubs nodded toward the west. "We trail these horses over the ridge. Cut that Injun sign and foller 'em."

"Follow them? I'd think we would want to go the other direction."

Brubs snorted. "You got some learnin' to do about Comanch, amigo. If nobody's chasin' them, they ain't gonna be lookin' behind 'em. They done been there." He picked up the slack in his bridle reins. "Besides, the tracks of them Injun horses'll help cover our trail. We foller 'em a couple miles, then turn west. A few days from now we'll be swillin' a cool *cerveza* down in Mexico, happy as ticks on a hound." He touched the spurs to Squirrel. "I'll ride point."

Dave was beginning to wonder just how far Brubs intended to ride point.

The sun had already started dropping toward the western horizon, and still the stocky Texan pushed on. The horses were as trail-weary and gaunt in the flanks as Willoughby was. They had, he figured, been on the move at a fast walk for better than ten hours and more than forty miles since the near encounter with the Indians. Even Willoughby's coyote dun, possibly the toughest horse ever bred in Texas, was feeling the effects of the brutal pace. The dun carried his head low and stumbled from time to time. The normal cream color of the gelding's skin was dark with sweat and streaked with lather where reins or saddle skirts touched his hide.

There was no shade, no escape from the pounding sun. The thick stands of scrub oak along the West Nueces had thinned as they traveled, first south along the distinct trail left by the Indian raiding party, then west into the barren and windswept region known as Mustang Desert. Even the mesquites were fewer now, stunted by drought and competing with Spanish dagger, cactus, and prickly pear to draw a bit of moisture from the thin and sandy soil.

The crossing at Devil's River near noontime had been the last watering hole. The country immediately ahead, partly shrouded by wind-blown dust and shimmering heat waves, outwardly promised no relief from thirst. The color of the land ranged from pale sand to washed-out brown. The scattered mesquites, occasional greasewood bushes, and infrequent junipers offered the only tint of heat-jaded green to the barren landscape.

Willoughby tried to ignore the weariness in his bones, the cottony taste in his mouth, and the sting of windwhipped sand against his stubbled cheeks. He had even begun to feel somewhat at home; for the first time since the raid on the Seguin ranch, he recognized landmarks here and there. He and Brubs had prowled the Mustang Desert country numerous times in their earlier hunts for the wild horses that thrived by the thousands in the seemingly lifeless countryside.

Four or five miles ahead, the flat desert floor gave way to upthrust ridges of craggy sandstone. Beyond the barren ridges were scattered springs and even a few natural watering holes called *abrevaderos,* or "watering troughs" in Spanish, where occasional storms filled hollowed depressions in flat benches and tables of sandstone.

Willoughby glanced up from his near stupor as Brubs rode back alongside. "We'll set a spell once we hit them water holes up in the hills. These horses is lookin' a tad trail-worn and gaunt in the flanks."

"They aren't the only ones." Willoughby had trouble getting the words out. Tongues didn't work well without spit. He reached for his canteen and shook it. Only a light gurgle sounded.

"Might want to hold off takin' that drink for an hour or so, partner," Brubs said, "just on the chance them tanks is dry."

Willoughby leveled a bloodshot glare at him.

"You are truly a comfort to a man, Brubs McCal-lan."

Brubs said, "Don't you fret none. I'd bet a battle of the best whiskey in Mexico there's water up there. Course, there could be some Injuns there, too. Maybe some Mex bandits. Let's trot on up there and take a look-see."

"What about the horses?"

Brubs shrugged. "Old Choctaw knows where we're headed. He's been in this country most of his life. He'll lead this bunch to the tanks." He reined his lathered sorrel around. "Come on, partner. We got a spot of scoutin' to do."

An hour later the coyote dun struggled the last few feet to the crest of the highest point on the rocky ridge and stopped, sides heaving, beside Brubs's sorrel. Willoughby stared toward the depressions carved in the rock shelves below. Sunlight glared from pools of rainwater that trickled down the rows of sandstone benches. There was no sign of human habitation around the pools.

Willoughby removed his hat, wiped a sweaty sleeve across his brow, and licked his lips. "Now that," he said, "is one beautiful sight."

"Matter of opinion," Brubs said.

Willoughby glanced at him. The Texan was staring toward the northeast along their back trail. His jaw was clenched. "What's a matter of opinion?"

Brubs raised a stubby finger and pointed. "Seen somethin' movin' out there, just north of that big cactus patch we rode past a spell back."

He let the hand drop. "You got better eyes than me. See anything?"

Willoughby squinted through the glare of late afternoon sun. He sat the saddle for a moment, his gaze drifting slowly over the landscape. A distant speck caught his attention. The speck seemed to split into three. One came straight ahead, the other two fanned out to the north and south. "Looks like horsemen," Willoughby said. "Three of them, I think."

"That's what I thought, too." Brubs spat and wiped his lips with the back of his hand. "Spotted their camp fire a couple times since we left the West Nueces."

"What do you make of it? Indians?"

"Nope. Three Injuns wouldn't be follerin' our trail like that. Thirty, maybe, but not three."

"Our trail?"

Brubs paused for a moment, shading his eyes with his hand, then sighed. "I was a bettin' man, partner, I'd bet that's a posse on our tail."

"Pettibone's men?"

Brubs shook his head. "Pettibone don't have three men could follow the trail we left. I ain't real sure who that is, but they're good. Damn good. And that's what's got this little worry worm to squirmin' in my biscuit pouch."

Willoughby turned to glare at Brubs. "You've known for days there was someone after us, and you didn't say a word to me about it. Why?"

Brubs shrugged. "Since you're all the time slippin' into snits over some little somethin' that ain't worth worryin' about, I didn't figure to fret you over it. Figured we'd lose 'em easy enough. Still can. We got us thirty, forty miles of hardpan, rock, badlands, and rivers to lose 'em in. You just leave it to old Brubs McCallan. I ain't even got serious about hidin' a trail yet. Won't be no problem."

"Whenever you say that, Brubs, it gets my own set of worry worms to wriggling." He sighed. "So what do we do now?"

"Water some horses, rest up a few hours, and then do us some heavy ridin', partner."

Dave Willoughby hated rivers.

He figured he had earned the right. He had never learned to swim, he had almost drowned in a flash flood on the Rio Grande, and nearly been sucked under the quicksands of the Atascosa.

"What the hell do you mean, we're riding *up-river?*"

Brubs, one leg hooked casually over his saddle horn said, "Best way to cover a trail, just in case those jaspers back there track us over the hardpan. Now, I don't reckon even old Liver-Eatin' Johnston could follow the tracks we laid the last couple days, but we might as well play us a hole card just in case."

Willoughby's fingers went cold. The Pecos was twenty yards wide, the water swift, and the streambed flanked by steep, rocky bluffs. "And the river is the hole card?"

"Yep. We just foller her upstream a few miles, then duck out into the canyon country, lay a few more false trails, then head south to Mexico."

Willoughby stared forlornly at the swirling waters of the Pecos. "I guess you're going to tell me there's nothing to it. Just a Sunday buggy ride or some such."

"That's a surefire fact, partner. Nothin' to give yourself the vapors over. Only thing you got to watch is there might be some deep holes here and there."

"That," Willoughby said sarcastically, "makes me feel just a whole lot better."

Brubs shifted his weight in the saddle. "Well, sometimes it comes one of them floods like back on the Rio —"

"You are a true comfort, Brubs McCallan. A true comfort."

"But it ain't likely. Ain't rained around here for nigh on to a month." He turned his head and spat. "Might have come a few storms upriver. Can't never tell about that. Seen a wall of water come down the Canadian one time, ten-foot high if it was an inch, and it hadn't rained in the Panhandle for six months. But don't fret it none."

"Don't fret it none," Willoughby parroted. He lifted his gaze to the sky. "He leads me into Indians, outlaws, cuckolded husbands, enraged fathers, bandits, bullets, posses, wild horses, knives, quicksand, floods, scorpions, rattlesnakes, and barroom brawls. And all the time this character I'm stuck with says don't fret it none."

"Don't go gettin' in one of them snits now, partner. We ain't goin' but four, five miles up-stream." Brubs nodded toward the roan under Willoughby's saddle. "Good thing you changed ponies this mornin'. Old Choctaw's a better river horse than that black or the coyote dun, and you're ridin' point."

"What! Why me?"

"Just doin' you a favor, partner. Figured you was gettin' tired of eatin' dust ridin' drag."

Willoughby glared at Brubs. "Favors. From you I don't need more favors. John Fletcher was right. About Texas and about you. He wrote, 'Death hath so many doors to let out life.' "

Brubs frowned. "This Fletcher feller had a point, at that. Might've met him once. He one of them Fletchers from over by Austin?"

"I seriously doubt it. He died in 1625."

"Reckon that explains how come we never said howdy, then." Brubs unhooked his knee from the horn and settled into the saddle. "These ponies have watered enough. Let's get 'em movin'. Don't worry, partner. If anything was to happen I'd sure try my best to find what was left of you."

"Thanks a hell of a lot."

"That's what partners is for." Brubs reined Mouse toward the back of the remuda, whistling "The Bonnie Blue Flag." Off-key.

"One thing's for certain," Willoughby muttered, "if the outcome of the war had depended on Brubs McCallan's musical ability, the Union would have won overnight and without a drop of blood spilled." He steeled himself, gripped the saddle horn so tight his knuckles were white, and kneed Choctaw toward the stream.

EIGHT

Brubs lay belly down on the rim of the steep peak in the rugged Glass Mountains and silently searched his vocabulary of profanity for a word he hadn't already used several times in the last four days.

Three horsemen rode slowly through the winding canyon three-quarters of a mile below the tip of the peak. Brubs had watched at first in hope when the trackers had lost the trail, and then in disgust as they picked it up again. It hadn't taken them long.

"I thought you told me you were an expert at hiding a track," Willoughby said at his side.

"Dammit, there ain't but one man alive could stick on a track like that," Brubs grumbled, a touch of admiration in his tone. "We bust our butts leavin' switchbacks and back tracks over rock and hardpan, up rivers, through mustang cavvys, through chaparral and cactus thickets a rabbit couldn't sneak through, a gully-washer of a rainstorm — and we ain't slowed him down by the length of a good spit." He studied the three horsemen intently for a moment, then sighed. "At least we're gettin' got by the best, partner. See that man out front, the one on the big dun horse? Wearin' that little town derby?"

"What about him?"

"That there, Dave, is bad news packin' a star.

135

That's Texas Ranger Sergeant Tobin Jamison."

"Where do you know this sergeant from?"

Brubs pursed his lips and spat. "He rode through Fredericksburg while you was laid up. I figgered he'd cleared the country a long time before we hit old man Pettibone's place."

"So what do we do now? Give ourselves up?"

Brubs cut a quick glance at Willoughby. "Not by no stretch. Jamison don't hold much by judges and juries. And he sure as sin don't like horse thieves. If he was feelin' the milk o' human kindness, he'd shoot us on the spot. If he wasn't, he'd hang us soon's he could find a tree taller'n you are." He sighed heavily. "Damn, it's getting so ain't no way a man can make a honest livin' anymore."

"Are you headed toward something," Willoughby said, "or just riding around the herd?"

Brubs muttered another curse. "We got to leave old man Pettibone's horses and cut out on our own. I figure Jamison's after them horses more'n he's after us."

Willoughby lifted an eyebrow. "I never thought I'd hear you admit someone had bested you, Brubs McCallan. I never thought I'd hear you say quit."

"We ain't quittin'. We're just backin' off a bit. Startin' right now." Brubs crabbed backward, away from the lip of the peak. Willoughby followed.

The two stopped, winded, at the bottom of the steep, shaley trail where Brubs's sorrel and Dave's black waited. After a moment, Brubs caught his breath. "We got a spell before Jamison tracks us all the way around the mountain to this canyon. We'll take our personal horses and put a bunch of miles between us and him before sundown." He paused for a moment to stare at the stolen horses cropping the scant grass in the canyon floor. "Damn, them's the best horses I ever stole. Sure hate to let 'em go."

Willoughby toed the stirrup and swung into the saddle. "As you've said before, we can always get more horses, Brubs. Let's ride. I have no intention of tangling with a Texas Ranger. Especially this one."

"Maybe," Brubs said thoughtfully as he mounted, "we could steal 'em back while Jamison's trailin' 'em back to Seguin?"

"That would most likely mean a shoot-out with three men who are very good with guns, Brubs," Dave said. "I didn't come to Texas to kill a Ranger. Forget it."

Brubs shrugged. "I reckon you're right this time, partner. I got to admit you're takin' this little setback pretty good."

"Riding with you, Brubs McCallan," Willoughby said wryly, "I've had plenty of practice at dealing with setbacks. Let's go."

Brubs kneed Squirrel into a trot toward camp. "Hell, we can steal some ponies from some rich ranchero down in Mexico." The familiar grin flashed. "Maybe we can still spend a little time with them señoritas. I know these two cute little

137

gals in Sonora —"

Willoughby cast a scathing glance at him. "For once get your mind off petticoats and liquor and show me just how good a trail you can't leave."

"Don't go gettin' fretty on me, Dave. Once Jamison gets them horses, we don't have no worries about hidin' our tracks."

Willoughby pulled the sweaty roan to a stop near the crest of a rocky ridge, glanced over his shoulder at their back trail, and glowered at Brubs. "What was that you said about no worries over hiding our tracks?"

Brubs turned to look at the three horsemen less than a mile behind. "How the hell was I to know they'd just ride on past that cavvy and come after us? God, I never seen such a stubborn man in my life as that Jamison."

"I hate to bring this up right now," Willoughby said, "but it appears that they are gaining ground on us."

Brubs's mouth set in a grim line. "Won't be for long," he said. "Ain't but a hundred miles or so to the Rio, and I got a few trail tricks left in me. Now, hush up and let's do some serious ridin'."

"Damn," Brubs said in awe, "that son of a bitch is *good!*"

Willoughby twisted in the saddle. The effort was almost more than he could manage. He had never been so exhausted in his life. Two nights and three days in the saddle, stopping only to change horses — and the Rangers were still on their trail, three determined lumps in the distance, moving steadily beneath the thick layer of heavy clouds that almost touched the tops of the mountains.

"Don't they ever get tired? Don't they ever get hungry? Don't they ever rest them horses?"

"I don't know about them, Brubs," Willoughby said, "but I'm not sure I can stay in the saddle another mile. Where is the Rio Grande, anyway? We should have reached it yesterday."

Brubs said, "Can't rightly say, partner."

Willoughby stiffened. "What do you mean, you can't rightly say?"

"Well, they wasn't no sun today, no stars last night. Just clouds. I done such a good job of hidin' our trail, I sort of got a mite confused."

"You got *lost?*"

"Mighty rugged country out here. Sun come up in the west yesterday, just before them clouds moved in, and it's been mixed up ever since. Sure wish it'd make up its mind." He turned and stared toward a distant peak. "Seems to me like I seen that hill from this side a couple days ago."

Willoughby moaned aloud.

"Now, Dave, don't you go gettin' fretty on me. Come daylight, I'll get my bearin's again — well, I'll be damned."

"What?"

"He bit. Jamison finally made a mistake." Brubs jabbed a finger toward the barely discernible horsemen. "He took that false trail I laid six hours ago." He turned to grin at Willoughby. "By the time he figgers out he's on a cold track it'll be full dark, and no moon tonight. He won't have no choice but to camp till sunup when it's light enough to read sign. By God, the man's human after all."

"That's a comfort. I was beginning to wonder. What now, O Great Pathfinder?"

Brubs tiptoed in the stirrups and looked around, then nodded to his left. "That hill over there. I seen somethin' when we rode past, like a cave mouth. We're lucky, it might have some water in it. We'll hole up there a few hours. Old Squirrel here needs hisself a nap." He leaned over and patted the sorrel's shoulder. "Poor old horse is just about done in."

"Squirrel," Willoughby said softly, "is not the only one. Let's go see if we can find that cave. Right now, that sounds better than the finest hotel in Chicago."

They almost missed the cave mouth in the near darkness. It was little more than a fissure in the rocks, thirty feet up from the base of the steep hill, the entrance partially screened by a heavy juniper growth. The horses were winded by the time they made the third switchback in the faint trail up the hillside and reached the cave.

The opening was just wide enough to admit a saddled horse; Willoughby had to strip the pack from the black and do some serious coaxing before the snorting gelding stepped gingerly through the narrow fissure.

Inside, the cave widened abruptly. It was tall enough for a man to stand and stretch, wide and deep enough to accommodate four horses and two men with space to spare. The air was damp and cool. And it had water, a steady drip into a shallow pool near the back wall. A deadfall of juniper twigs and limbs just outside the mouth would provide plenty of fuel for a small fire.

"Never seen a hole in a hill look so cozy," Brubs said as he massaged his backside. "Now I know how a badger feels when he comes home. Anything left in the possibles sack?"

Willoughby opened the drawstring and peered inside. "Enough coffee for one pot now and one in the morning, a handful of dried apples, and a few strips of bacon and jerky each."

"Sounds better than prime steak and fine whiskey," Brubs said happily. "I'll take care of the horses. Wrestle a few sticks from that deadfall out front. We'll build us a little fire."

Willoughby stepped outside the cave and glanced around. He was slightly surprised to find that darkness was falling so quickly. The clouds overhead had broken, letting a bit of lingering gray sunset light filter onto the countryside. Beyond the screen of junipers, the site partway up the canyon wall overlooked a wide section of reasonably flat valley. It would, he thought, provide an excellent field of fire, should that become necessary. A handful of good riflemen could stand off an attack as long as their food and ammunition lasted. And with a good three-pounder rifled fieldpiece here, no opposing force could mount a frontal attack.

Willoughby silently swore at himself and tried to push the thoughts aside. He told himself he had to quit thinking like an artillery battery commander. But old habits died hard. Even habits that had been tempered with loathing for the big, noisy guns that sprayed shell and shrapnel over and into strangers he didn't know and didn't particularly want to hurt in the first place.

He scrounged in the deadfall. It was almost pitch-black by the time he found an armful of dry limbs and twigs that would burn fast without making a lot of smoke. He paused to study the night sky. Through a break in the clouds the North Star showed crisp and clear for an instant. It didn't seem to be in the right place, but Willoughby accepted it as fact. At least now he knew which way was north. He was about to return to the cave when a point of light caught his eye. He stood for a moment, staring toward the southeast, then directly east. A second faint dot flared in the distance.

Willoughby stopped at the narrow cave entrance and called to Brubs.

"What is it, partner?" Brubs said as he stepped into the clear.

"Didn't those three Rangers stay together when they took the false trail you laid?"

"Sure did. Why?"

"There are two camp fires out there." He

shifted the firewood to the crook of an elbow and pointed out the lights with his free hand. "One there. Another there. About three miles apart. What do you make of it?"

Brubs stared toward the distant light points for a moment. "We know who's at one of 'em. Jamison. Other one could be a vaquero camp. Maybe a sheepherder." He snorted in disgust. "Damn country's gettin' so crowded a man can't ride a hundred miles without stumblin' over somebody." He shrugged. "Ain't no worry of ours, nohow. Clouds are breakin' up. Come daylight we'll put the sun on our left and move out. By supper time we'll be in Mexico." He turned toward the cave. "Let's eat and grab some soogan time. My tuckered's hangin' out."

Dave Willoughby rode relaxed in the saddle, the midmorning sun warm on his shoulders. A few hours sleep hadn't chased all the exhaustion, but it had helped.

Brubs, riding alongside, turned in the saddle and said to him, "We got her made, partner. Couple more hours, we'll hit the Rio and be in Mexico."

Willoughby frowned. "How do we know Jamison won't cross the river?"

"Mexico's not his bailiwick. He don't have no authority there. And if he crosses over and runs into some *federales*, he could start a war 'tween the States and Mexico. That sure as hell wouldn't help his chances at making lieutenant."

"How will we live in Mexico? We have no money, no provisions, and no prospects for employment."

Brubs shook his head as they neared the top of a low ridge in the river breaks. "Dave, you're gonna fret yourself plumb into an early grave. Don't you worry none. It'll work out. Just trust old Brubs —" He abruptly yanked the gray mustang to a stop and barked a soft curse.

"What is it?"

"Injuns. That same bunch of bronco Comanches we snuck past a few days back. Comin' this way." Brubs reined Mouse toward a clump of mesquite and broken boulders at the base of the ridge. He motioned for Willoughby to follow.

The two reached the cover of the rocks and brush only moments before the Comanche cavalcade moved into view. They were less than two hundred yards away, headed north. Willoughby tensed as the procession passed. He counted twenty braves, most of them armed with repeating rifles, a few with handguns, their faces painted and horses decorated with the spoils of war. Bolts of calico torn into strips were tied into the manes and tails of the war ponies; one brave wore a long swatch of blue cloth wrapped around his body like a Roman toga. Fresh scalps fluttered from the muzzles of rifles and bridles of horses. It was the first time Willoughby had ever seen a wild Indian up close. The sight chilled his blood.

Brubs sat tensely, rifle across the pommel of

his saddle, thumb on the hammer. He glanced at Willoughby and signaled for silence.

Willoughby felt the black stir under him, as if the horse were about to whicker, and he tugged sharply on the reins. The horse quieted down.

It seemed to Willoughby that half the day had passed before the last Indian disappeared from view around the back side of the ridge. Still, Brubs made no move to leave the cover of rocks and brush until another quarter hour had elapsed. Then he motioned to Willoughby and kneed Mouse free of the hiding place.

"Never thought I'd be glad to see Injuns," Brubs muttered. "Them Comanch'll give Jamison somethin' to worry about besides us."

"How can you be so sure of that? We don't even know where Jamison is."

Brubs squinted along the back trail. "He's about a mile behind us." He leaned over and spat. "He's follerin' our tracks from the cave. That's gonna lead him right into a nest of Injuns, looks like. Keep him busy long enough we can get across the Rio." He touched the spurs to Mouse. "Come on, partner. Mexico's a-waitin'."

The two had ridden less than a half mile before the distant report of the first gunshot reached their ears. Several others followed on the heels of the first; Willoughby thought he heard a high-pitched cry, something like the Rebel yell, amid the crackle of gunfire.

Brubs pulled his horse to a stop, lifted in the

stirrups, and gazed along the back trail for several heartbeats.

"Brubs," Willoughby said softly, "those Rangers are outnumbered better than six to one."

Brubs shifted his gaze to Willoughby. "Are you thinkin' what I'm thinkin', partner?"

Willoughby swallowed. "I'm afraid so." He felt the cold sweat break out on his forehead.

Brubs sighed heavily. "Hell, we can't just ride off and leave no white men to get burnt over a slow fire by some damn Comanche. Even if the white men is tryin' to hang us." He cracked the action of the old Henry to make sure a cartridge was chambered, then looked at Willoughby. "Partner," Brubs said, "we are six different kinds of fool."

"The thought," Willoughby said as he slipped his rifle from the saddle scabbard "had crossed my mind."

"Aw, hell. No man lives forever. Let's go." Brubs spurred Mouse toward the sounds of battle.

Brubs checked the gray on a low hill overlooking the battleground below. The Comanche war party had formed up in a semicircle a quarter of a mile from the three men trapped in a shallow depression. The Rangers were almost obscured by gun smoke and dust. One of the white men seemed to be down; the bodies of three Comanches lay in the stunted bunchgrass and sand. A line of mesquite trees flanked the basin a hundred yards from the battle site. The trailing edge of the hill twisted back to within fifty yards of the Indian skirmish line.

Brubs reached into a saddlebag and dumped a box of cartridges into his shirt pocket. "Them Comanch are fixin' to ride a circle around the Ranger boys. Comanch thinks that if he can ride around an enemy he'll make a magic circle that the enemy can't get through. We got to bust them Comanches' medicine." He pointed toward the line of mesquites. "You take them trees over there," he said his jaw set, a grim expression in his eyes. "I'll spur around to the edge of this hill. We'll have 'em in a cross fire. You got a better idea?"

Willoughby shook his head. "Not unless you've got a brace of six-pounder cannon in your saddlebag."

"Let's ride. Watch your hair, partner."

Willoughby reined his black from the hill into the thin cover of mesquites, the crackle of gunshots and whoops of the Comanches loud in his ears as he weaved his way to the end of the thicket. He yanked the gelding to a sliding stop and bailed out of the saddle. He flipped the reins over a mesquite limb and sprinted, half crouching, to the edge of the trees. He had barely settled in when one of the Indians lifted his rifle and waved it in a circle over his head. A chorus of high-pitched yelps swept the Comanche ranks; the Indians at each end of the half circle quirted their mounts into a charge.

Willoughby forced himself to stay calm, to calculate the range and line the sights. He didn't fire at the Indian who swept by broadside before him; he waited until the warrior turned his horse to circle the trapped men, presenting his back at a quartering angle. Then Willoughby squeezed the trigger.

The Indian jerked upright, then slumped over the neck of his pony. Willoughby levered another round into the chamber, lined the sights on the chest of a startled warrior who had yanked his pony to a stop, and squeezed off the round. The Indian tumbled over the rump of his horse.

Willoughby heard the snap of a slug beside his ear. Twigs and fallen leaves peppered his cheek. Two Indians yanked mounts from the circle and charged toward him. He snapped a quick shot, missed, and frantically worked the Winchester's action. They were almost on him when he heard the whack of lead on flesh. One of the Indians grunted and fell, hit by a shot from one of the Rangers. Willoughby whipped the muzzle of his rifle into line and yanked off a hurried shot. The slug hit the second Indian's pony in the chest. The war pony staggered and went down. Willoughby took his time, lined the sights, and shot the Comanche in the head.

He thumbed cartridges into the loading port of the Winchester. Over the heavier crack of Ranger rifles Willoughby heard the lighter pop of Brubs's .44 rimfire. Through the swirling dust and powder smoke, Willoughby saw two more Indians go down, caught in the storm of lead from the Rangers in the center and the two un-expected rifles at their flanks.

The Indian attack broke. Warriors quirted mounts away from the fight. Two Indians swept toward a downed warrior, scooped the injured man up by an arm, and swung him up behind a Comanche on a buckskin mustang. Willoughby snapped a shot at the fleeing horsemen. The slug fell short.

A sudden, almost eerie, silence fell over the battle site. For an instant, Willoughby felt as if he were back on the killing fields of Antietam and the Wilderness. Battles rarely tapered off in sporadic shooting; they just stopped. The silence was unsettling. A gust of breeze swept the last wisp of gun smoke and dust from the shallow basin below. The fight had lasted only two or three minutes after he and Brubs joined in, but it seemed to Willoughby that hours had passed. Several Indians lay in the sandy soil, four still and unmoving. One was trying to crawl away dragging useless legs along with his elbows. Another sat dazed, hands clasped around a bullet wound in his gut. A Ranger in a derby hat stood, leveled his rifle, and shot the crawling Comanche in the back. The Indian shuddered once and went still. A second Ranger plunked a slug through the skull of the gut-shot Indian. The echoes of the final shot of the battle rolled through the rugged hills.

Willoughby realized he was sweating profusely; the fore stock of the Winchester was slick and difficult to grip. He knelt at the edge of the thicket, wondering if he were going to be sick. Willoughby didn't know if it was revulsion at killing or pure, raw terror that tore at his gut. The wave of nausea finally passed.

"Dave, you all right? You hit?" Brubs's question was sharp and clear in the sudden quiet. Willoughby hadn't even heard the Texan ride up behind him in the thicket. Brubs even had the packhorses in tow.

Willoughby tried to reply, got out only a strangled croak and swallowed hard before he could say, "I'm all right." He forced himself to his feet. His knees felt weak and shaky.

"You don't look so hot, partner," Brubs said, a slight grin on his face.

"I tend to get choked on powder smoke," Willoughby said. "Especially when somebody's shooting at me." He reached for the black's reins. "What do we do now? You think the Rangers will just let us ride off?"

Brubs said, "Dave, you don't know Texas Rangers. They'll be back on our tails as soon as they can mount up. But there's one place they sure ain't gonna be lookin' for us."

"Where's that?"

"In their own camp."

"What?"

"We're gonna join the Rangers, partner. Always wondered what it'd be like to be a lawman, 'specially one huntin' horse thieves."

Willoughby stared at Brubs in disbelief. "You

150

must have taken a slug through the brain, friend."
He sighed. "On second thought, it wouldn't have
hit much. I guess you have it all planned out?"

"Sure do, partner. When a man's got you cold,
best thing to do is chunk a few horse apples at
him. I'm fixin' to fling a few. You leave everything up to old Brubs. Just foller my lead." He
rode to the edge of the thicket. "You boys down
there! Easy on them triggers! We ain't wearin'
feathers! Okay to ride in?"

"Come ahead," the call came back.

Brubs waited until Willoughby mounted, then
handed over the reins of the pack animals and
kneed Mouse toward the three men in the depression.

"You boys all right down here?" Brubs said as
he pulled the gray to a stop before the Rangers.
"Anybody hit?"

The ranger in the derby nodded toward one
of the men. "Casey lost a little chunk of leg. It
doesn't appear to be anything serious. Where did
you two come from?"

Brubs pointed a thumb toward the south.
"Down yonder a ways. We was chasin' a couple
horse thieves. Crossed fresh Injun sign a few
minutes before the shootin' started. Thought
somebody mighta needed a hand."

"We did. We're obliged to you." The Ranger's
tone was cordial, but the expression in the pale
blue eyes was considerably cooler than his words.
"If you hadn't flanked those Comanches, we
could have been in for a long day." The lawman

151

finally strode to Brubs's stirrup and offered a hand. "Tobin Jamison. Texas Rangers," he said.

Brubs took the hand. "Brubs McCallan. Texas Horsetradin' Company." He released Jamison's hand and nodded in Willoughby's direction. "My partner, Dave Willoughby."

Jamison nodded to Willoughby, then said to Brubs, "These horse thieves you were after. Did you catch up to them?"

Brubs shook his head. "Nah. They got across the Rio on us just about the time we cut that Injun sign. I figger they're halfway to Sonora by now. We give 'em a good run, though. Tracked 'em damn near all the way from San 'Tone."

Jamison nodded, but his expression was still guarded and suspicious. "Why don't you boys set a spell? We'll get some coffee brewed while Casey patches up his leg."

Brubs dismounted. "Sounds mighty fine to me. We been runnin' low on grub the last few days." He turned to Willoughby. "Light and set, partner."

Willoughby hesitated, his gaze darting around the battleground and the Indian bodies. "What if the Indians come back?"

"They won't," Jamison said. "They lost a lot of war medicine here today." He racked the action of his Winchester, then started feeding cartridges into the loading port. "They'll sneak back to the reservation for now. Probably come back in a few days or weeks to retrieve the bones of their dead." Jamison shrugged. "Comanches won't press a fight unless they have superior numbers and a good chance to win without suffering many losses. They may be savages, but they're not stupid."

Willoughby reluctantly dismounted.

Jamison waved a hand toward the other two Rangers. "The one with the ouch on his leg is Casey Sinclair. The tall one's Lee Denton."

Sinclair looked up from bandaging his leg long enough to nod a greeting. He was medium height, thick in the chest and shoulders, with eyes almost as black as printer's ink in a face tanned the color of old leather by wind and sun. If Sinclair felt any pain, Willoughby thought, he certainly wasn't showing it. A tough man.

Denton offered a hand. He was almost as tall as Willoughby and nearly as lean, shaggy blond hair spilling past his collar. His eyes were a strange color, Willoughby noted — almost the amber of a mountain lion's. His grip was dry and firm. "Obliged for the help, boys," Denton said. "It was getting a mite antsy around here for a while. I'll go rustle us up some firewood."

Willoughby loosened the cinches on the saddle horses and eased the straps on the packs, then squatted by the small fire and waited for the coffee water to heat. He couldn't shake the uneasy feeling in his gut. Brubs and Denton were already swapping horse yarns like two old school buddies meeting for the first time in years. Sinclair still hadn't said a word.

"McCallan, we might have a problem here,"

Jamison said. He still held the Winchester in the crook of an arm. His blue eyes were locked on Brubs's face.

"What might that be?"

"Those horses you boys rode in on." Jamison's tone went hard and cold. "Their tracks look mighty familiar."

Brubs's brows went up in an innocent expression. "How so?"

"Those tracks," Jamison said, "are the hoofprints we've been following for days. The tracks of the two horse thieves we're after."

NINE

Dave Willoughby hadn't even seen Casey Sinclair move, but all of a sudden he was looking down the barrel of a cocked Winchester.

Willoughby glanced at Brubs. The Texan stood stockstill, not a muscle moving, and for good cause — the muzzle of Ranger Sergeant Tobin Jamison's rifle was about two inches from Brubs's left ear. Lee Denton stood to one side, long legs flexed at the knees, his right hand on the butt of the Colt Peacemaker at his hip.

"You boys are under arrest," Jamison said, his tone cold. "The charge is horse theft."

Willoughby's gut tied itself in a knot. The black eyes looking at him over the Winchester sights held a calm, almost disinterested, expression. It was a spooky look.

"Don't take it personally," Jamison said. "It's not that I don't appreciate what you fellows did here today, maybe saving our scalps from a Comanche knife. But I've got a job to do." He never took his eyes from Brubs. "Lee, relieve these men of their weapons."

Willoughby tried to ignore the signals his bladder was suddenly sending as Denton slipped Willoughby's Colt from its holster and tucked it in his waistband.

A sudden whoop of laughter sliced through the growing tension. Willoughby glanced at Brubs.

The Texan was bent over, slapping his leg and howling in glee. Willoughby didn't see the humor in the situation.

"What's so funny?" Jamison didn't sound amused, either.

Brubs raised a hand, gasping for air between laughs. Tears trickled down his cheeks. "Gimme . . . a minute . . ." The statement ended in another fit of whoops punctuated by hiccups, snorts, and giggles.

"I never saw a man quite so tickled over getting himself hanged," Jamison said.

Lee Denton appeared to be trying to stifle the hint of a grin as he lifted Brubs's pistol from its holster. Willoughby had to admit that in shotgun terms, Brubs McCallan had about an eight-gauge laugh. It was hard not to catch it when it went off at close range.

Brubs swiped a hand across the tear tracks on his cheeks. "You mean to tell me — that you boys — been trackin' *us?*" The question set Brubs into another full-bore howl of mirth. After a moment the storm passed. Brubs got his wind back. "You talk about a Mexican circus? Hell, we was trackin' them horse thieves and you was trackin' us. Damnedest thing I ever seen."

Jamison still wasn't amused. "What the hell are you trying to pull, McCallan?"

"You know what's really got my tickle box down side up, Jamison? There for a couple miles back on the Pecos, Willoughby and me was trackin' *you!*" Brubs dissolved into another hoot-

156

ing fit. "Ain't that somethin'? We was trackin' them horse thieves, you was trackin' us, and we was trackin' you! Like a dog a-chasin' its tail." He loosed another giggle.

The first hint of indecision flickered in Jamison's pale blue eyes. "You left the horses behind."

"Hell, yes, we did." Teeth flashed in a wide grin under Brubs's untrimmed, bushy mustache. "They wasn't *our* horses, Jamison! I reckon we got to pushin' them damn rustlers so hard they figured to leave most of the nags behind, thinkin' we'd quit the trail once we had 'em back."

Jamison stared hard and long into Brubs's eyes, as if trying to read something there. Finally, he sighed and lowered the rifle. "McCallan," Jamison said, "I don't know whether you're telling it straight or not. But if you're yarning me, you spin a mighty fine tale and I admire a good liar. It *could* have happened like that."

The grin finally broke through Denton's resolve. He chuckled, deep in his throat, but checked the laugh at a sharp glance from Jamison. Sinclair's expression hadn't changed. Neither had the angle of the Winchester muzzle pointed at the bridge of Willoughby's nose.

Jamison turned to Sinclair. "Lower the rifle, Casey. We aren't going to shoot anybody." He paused for emphasis and then added, "Yet."

Willoughby breathed a sigh of relief when the rifle muzzle dropped.

"Say, Jamison, didn't you mention somethin'

about coffee a spell back?" Brubs pointed toward the fire as if nothing — like almost getting lynched — had happened in the past few minutes. "That stuff boils any longer we'll be able to cast forty-five slugs out of it."

Jamison nodded. "All right, go ahead and fetch your mess kits. Then I'll decide what to do with you two."

Brubs and Willoughby sat cross-legged beside the fire and waited for the rims of their tin cups to cool enough for a sip at the scalding hot coffee.

"Jamison, I been thinkin'," Brubs said. "Seems like we all here got somethin' in common."

"Like what?"

"Horse thieves." Brubs sipped at his coffee and winced. "Pure pine tar. Good stuff." He licked his lips and said to Jamison, "When them rustlers left the cavvy behind, they didn't leave the two horses they swiped from us. They still got 'em. You plannin' on crossin' the Rio after them two?"

Jamison leveled a steady glare at Brubs. "Why?"

Brubs said, "Thought we might go with you. Could be you need a couple extra guns, you go into Mexico. Some sure 'nuff bad hombres down there."

Jamison lifted an eyebrow. "You would go into Mexico after them? For just two horses?"

"That's a plumb fact, Jamison," Brubs said earnestly. "Them was good horses. And Dave and me, we just flat can't abide horse thieves. We catch them two, we'll string 'em up from the nearest tree, I tell you that."

Jamison paused for a moment, his brow wrinkled in thought. "I can't cross the river. I have no authority to go into Mexico. In fact, I have specific orders not to."

Brubs sighed in resignation, then turned to Willoughby. "Guess we'll just have to go her alone, partner. Sure woulda been nice to have a couple Rangers along, though."

"I can't let you go, McCallan."

"How come? We ain't rustlers and we ain't lawmen. Just a couple of honest horse traders lookin' to get our property back."

Jamison frowned. "I can't let you go because I'm not totally convinced you're as innocent as you make it sound. I'm arresting you on suspicion of horse theft. We'll pick up those stolen horses on the way, then I'll take you back to Seguin along with them. If the bank clerk says you're not the men who jumped him, you'll be free to go."

Brubs shook his head. "Jamison, you are sure 'nuff one of the most untrustin' men I ever met." He swigged at his coffee. "Hell," he said, his tone downcast, "we can't go nowhere anyhow. We run out of grub two days ago and our horses is wore plumb down." He lifted his gaze to Willoughby. "Sorry, partner. I know that coyote dun was your favorite rope horse."

Willoughby shrugged, trying to make the effort look casual. "We don't want to fight the Rangers, Brubs. We'll do as Jamison says. I can get another horse."

Brubs clucked his tongue. "Damn shame, them rustlers gettin' away clean like that." His face suddenly brightened. "Got to give 'em credit, though. Them two could sure 'nuff hide a trail."

Jamison grunted. "They must have been. I never saw their tracks. Another reason I just might buy your yarn is that you boys sure weren't trying to hide your trail."

Brubs looked indignant. He opened his mouth as if to protest, but caught Willoughby's *shut-the-hell-up* look before the words came out. His lower lip drooped in an injured pout.

"Forget about it, Brubs," Willoughby said, hoping he sounded disappointed. "What's done is done. The rustlers got away."

Brubs sighed. "I reckon they did, but it sure itches my whiskers we didn't get to hang 'em. Like you say, what's done's done." He sipped at his cup. "Sure gonna be a long ride back. And I got my hungries up somethin' fierce, chousin' thieves and fightin' Injuns. You gonna feed us, Jamison?"

The Ranger nodded. "I may shoot a man from time to time, maybe even hang one once in a while. But I don't starve prisoners."

"Sergeant," Willoughby said, "are we formally under arrest?"

"Not formally. There has been no indictment issued for you as yet. But informally, yes. Either way, you will have an armed escort back to Seguin. And we're going to keep a close watch on you two along the way."

Brubs sulked for a moment, then suddenly snapped his fingers. "Say, Jamison, how's about we cut a deal here?"

Jamison frowned suspiciously. "What deal?"

"We ain't really under arrest, but you won't let us leave, neither. You say you got to keep an eye on us. Now, you know they's Injuns prowlin' this country. Bandits and rustlers is so thick you could stir 'em with a stick. Lots of places out here lawmen ain't special welcome. Could be you could use a couple more guns somewheres."

Jamison's cold blue eyes narrowed. "Why don't you just spit out what you're thinking, McCallan?"

"Why, it's as simple as an open door on a two-holer," Brubs said. "You swear us in as Rangers, give us our guns back, and we'll ride shotgun for you."

Jamison never blinked. "You are out of your mind, McCallan. No prisoners of mine, indicted or not, carry guns."

Brubs said, "Most unreasonablest man I ever met. Why not?"

"Two reasons. First, I don't trust you as far as I could throw a chuck wagon. Second, the Texas Rangers don't employ suspected horse thieves. Good enough for you?"

Brubs sighed in resignation. "I reckon. Don't know how you got to be such an untrustin' man, and I've knowed a Ranger or two in my time who wouldn't mind puttin' his saddle on another man's horse."

"Sergeant?"

161

"What, Willoughby?"

"If we do get jumped by rustlers or Indians, could we have our guns back then?"

"If that happens," Jamison said, "I'll hand the damn things to you myself. In the meantime, don't give us any trouble. Sinclair hasn't shot a white man in over a month now. He gets a little testy when that happens."

Brubs glanced at the dark-skinned man with the black eyes. "How come he don't talk?"

"Casey doesn't need to. He's got his own ways of letting his opinions be known." Jamison tossed out the dregs from his coffee cup. "Mount up, boys. I'd like to get to Horsehead Springs before sundown. We'll camp there tonight and gather some horses tomorrow."

Dave Willoughby leaned back against a fallen cottonwood tree, Brubs McCallan at his side, and drained the last swig from his coffee cup.

At last, Willoughby thought, Sergeant Jamison fed his prisoners well. Willoughby's belly was full for the first time in days, and not from jerky or stale bacon.

Brubs swiped the last of the fried venison grease and flour gravy from his tin plate with a remnant of biscuit and popped the morsel in his mouth. Brubs looked, Willoughby thought, like a man without a care in the world, happy as a horned toad in an ant bed. Willoughby looked up as Tobin Jamison strode to the fallen tree and looked the two over as carefully as if he were seeing them for the first time. "You boys get enough to eat?" he finally said.

Brubs nodded and mumbled something around the last bite of gravy bread.

"Yes, sir," Willoughby said. "It was quite good. Mr. Sinclair is an accomplished camp cook."

Jamison said, "You talk like a man with considerable education, Willoughby. How did you manage to get yourself tied up with some saddle tramp like McCallan?"

"Saddle tramp!" Brubs sprayed biscuit crumbs in the squawk of indignation. "You got no call insultin' a man like that, Jamison! I'm a businessman! Half owner of the Texas Horsetradin' Company, by God!"

Jamison cut a hard glance at Willoughby. "We'll find out for sure just what business you are really in as soon as we get back to Seguin, McCallan."

"Look, Jamison," Willoughby said, "that was uncalled-for." He was surprised at the touch of anger in his tone. "I won't tolerate any man insulting my friend. And that includes Texas Rangers."

The faintest of smiles touched Jamison's thin lips. "I admire a man who stands by his friends, Willoughby. Maybe I was out of line. Benefit of the doubt and all." He made no further apology. Jamison stared hard into Willoughby's face for a long moment. "You look familiar. I never forget a face or a description on a wanted poster. That bothers me some."

163

"Sergeant," Willoughby said lamely, "I don't believe we've ever met, and you won't find my description on any flyer."

Jamison shrugged. "It'll come to me. You men get some sleep. We've a lot of country to cover tomorrow."

"Jamison?"

"What now, McCallan?"

"You gonna shackle us? Man shouldn't take no chances with dangerous desperadoes like Dave and me."

"What would I need shackles for?" The Ranger's tone was slightly amused. "If you're innocent, you won't run. If you're guilty, you'll run. If you run, I'd have to report you as killed while trying to escape."

Brubs said, "I reckon your point is took."

"Besides," Jamison said, "where would you go? You're in the middle of nowhere, without weapons or supplies, and you'd be on foot. That dun horse of mine is trained to raise a ruckus if a stranger tries to take a mount from my picket line. In addition to which, all three of us are light sleepers. We usually wake up shooting if everything isn't as peaceful as a Sunday camp meeting." Jamison turned and walked away.

"That man," Brubs muttered in grudging respect, "is plumb made out of rawhide and bone. He's got us by the short hair, partner, and I got a strong notion he wasn't funnin' us none about that killed while tryin' to escape business. Happens a lot with Rangers." Brubs sighed. "I got to tell you, Dave, I ain't deep-down spooked of no man, but I'd just as leave not have no part of that hombre."

"So what do we do?"

"We ain't got no choice, way I see it," Brubs said softly. "We go back to Seguin."

"And if that clerk identifies us?"

"We share a limb someplace, partner." Brubs's soft words rode heavy in the early evening stillness of the Horsehead Springs camp. Finally, he said, "We just got to make sure he don't."

"How do we manage that?"

"First off, we was wearin' bandannas over our faces. Second, that old man's blind as a daylight bat. Then, he was so boogered he wouldn't of knowed his own mother." Brubs downed the last swallow from his coffee cup, leaned back, and scratched his ribs. "What we got to do ain't goin' to set well with you, partner."

Willoughby frowned. "I have become somewhat accustomed to those conditions. What do you have in mind?"

Brubs said, "You got to learn to like grubby, Dave. No shaves, no baths, no clothes changin' or hair trimmin' between here and Seguin for you. Me, I'll spruce up fancylike 'fore we get there, even if it ain't September yet. And you'll do all the talkin'."

Willoughby's upper lip twisted in a grimace. "What good will that do?"

"When a man can't see too good, he usual remembers smells and voices. Time we get back, you'll be ripe enough to make a man's eyes water and I'll be smellin' like the first rose of summer. That'll confuse his sniffer. And that funny back-East, college-boy talk of yours'd sure not set no warnin' bells off in his ears. You remember, I was the one done all the talkin' at the ranch."

Willoughby sighed. "What if Pettibone shows up?"

"That," Brubs said sincerely, "is somethin' I'd just as soon not think on." He picked up his tin plate and cup, then stood. "Let's get these here mess kits cleaned up, partner. I reckon I'm gonna sleep like a baby tonight."

Willoughby reined Choctaw to a stop on the ridge overlooking the valley in the Glass Mountains.

Pettibone's horses were nowhere in sight.

Brubs twisted in the saddle to face the Ranger on his right. "Wonder what happened to them horses? I wouldn't of thought they drifted much on account of this here's the best water and grass for a long ways around, and them broomtails was plumb wore down."

Lee Denton shifted a quarter-sized chunk of tobacco to his other cheek and spat, the glob skipping neatly between his bay horse's ears. "We'll find out soon enough. Any sign the sergeant can't read, Casey Sinclair can."

"That Sinclair's a downright spooky feller," Brubs said. "Lookin' into them beady little black eyes is like starin' at a mad rattler."

Denton worked his chew for a moment, then leaned over and spat. The amber stream hit a horned toad between the eyes. The diminutive lizard squatted, shook its head in indignation, then scurried for the cover of a prickly pear patch. "Any smart man who doesn't know Casey should be spooked at him," Denton said. "Second worse thing a man could do is make Jamison mad. Worst thing he could do is make Casey Sinclair mad."

Brubs cocked an eyebrow. "Where do you fit in that peckin' order, Denton?"

The Ranger shrugged. "Third." He lifted himself in the stirrups and stared at the horsemen in the valley. "Sinclair's got them. He's on the track."

The horsemen on the ridge watched in silence as Sinclair checked his horse, stared at the ground, then gestured to Jamison. The two conferred for a moment before trotting their horses back to the group waiting on the ridge.

"What's up, Sergeant?" Denton asked.

"Horse thieves. Looks like they took the whole remuda."

"Damn! Them was our horses!"

"Brubs —"

Brubs glanced at Willoughby, caught the almost imperceptible head shake, then turned back to Jamison. He could read the question and the challenge in the Ranger's eyes. "Sorry, Jamison. Didn't mean to bust in on you like that but these damned unethical horse thieves just plumb

167

scorches my drawers. I mean, it ain't right, after we spent so much time trackin' them two other thieves, and now we're right back where we started."

Jamison didn't look convinced, but he didn't push the point. He turned back to Denton. "Tracks say twelve men. Headed southwest, not more than five or six hours ago." The Ranger sergeant spat in disgust. "We must have passed within a mile of them. Looks like they're bound for Mexico."

Denton's amber eyes narrowed. "What's your pleasure, boss?"

Saddle leather creaked as Jamison shifted his weight. "We came after horse thieves and horses boys. The job isn't finished yet. Let's go." He reined his horse toward the southwest.

Casey Sinclair took the point, ranging well ahead on scout, glancing at the ground from time to time. They were moving at a fast trot. Brubs and Willoughby dropped back a few feet behind Jamison. Denton brought up the rear, his Winchester already unsheathed, the brass butt plate resting on a thigh.

"Dammit, Brubs," Willoughby whispered, "you have to watch your tongue, or you're going to get us hanged for sure."

"Sorry, partner," Brubs said. "That just sorta slipped out. We worked mighty hard for them horses. Ain't fair somebody else ought to get — Wait a minute! Didn't Jamison say twelve men?"

"He did."

Brubs's eyes narrowed. "Who do you know around these parts rides with a bunch that size? And got a taste for good horses?"

Willoughby rode in silence for a moment, his brow wrinkled in thought. Then his head snapped around. "Delgado."

"Couldn't be nobody else." Brubs's jaw was set, teeth clenched. He spurred Mouse into an easy lope and pulled up alongside Jamison's dun, Willoughby close behind. The dun backed its ears and bared its teeth. Mouse danced a cautious step away. "Jamison," Brubs said, "Willoughby and me think we know who took them horses."

The Ranger sergeant twisted in the saddle. "Who?"

"Gilbert Delgado, that's who. I'd sure like to drop a hammer on that damn pepper gut bandit."

"Why?"

"The son of a bitch stole our horses, that's why!"

Jamison's hand drifted to the Colt at his hip. "I thought you just said these horses weren't yours. That the men who stole your horses got away across the river."

"Sergeant," Willoughby broke in quickly, "Brubs doesn't mean this particular time or these particular horses. Delgado raided our camp when we were out mustanging several months back. He took our ponies and killed our friend, Stump Hankins."

"Yeah," Brubs muttered lamely, "that's what I meant."

169

Jamison's hand fell away from the pistol. "You could be right, McCallan. That could be Delgado out there. And if it is, I will be a happy man."

"You know Delgado, Sergeant?"

"I know of him, Willoughby. Delgado's name is on every wanted list from Aransas Pass to California." The Ranger's lips twisted in a scowl. "We'll find out soon enough. I know where he's headed. He's going through Hangtree Pass."

"Hangtree Pass?"

"Narrow gorge through the Chiniti Mountains upriver from Ojinaga. If I'm right, we can cut across the Cuesta del Burro range, ride the night out, and catch up to him about the time he reaches Hangtree."

Willoughby rode in silence for a moment. Finally, curiosity got the better of him. "Sergeant, why is this place called Hangtree Pass?"

"Dave, this ain't no time for a geography lesson," Brubs muttered.

"It's called that," Jamison said, "because of a big cottonwood tree at a spring on the south end of the pass. The cottonwood is just the right height for a hanging tree."

"Oh," Willoughby said. His throat muscles went tight at the thought.

"It's a fine tree for the purpose," Jamison said, admiration in his tone. "Lynched a couple of bandits there myself two, three years back. If you stand a man on his saddle, put the rope just right, then whack his horse on the rump, it breaks their necks clean as a whip every time."

Willoughby swallowed hard.

"Yes, sir," Jamison said, "the good Lord knew what he was doing when he put that tree there just so. He had the Texas Rangers and horse thieves in mind."

TEN

Texas Ranger Sergeant Tobin Jamison squatted on his heels in the fading sunset and let his gaze drift over the half circle of faces gathered around. Willoughby thought he saw a faint gleam of satisfaction in Jamison's pale blue eyes.

Casey Sinclair stood at Jamison's side, the bridle reins of a lathered brown gelding draped loosely over a forearm as he rolled a cigarette. Sinclair showed no sign of fatigue even though he had worn down two horses during a long day of hard riding on scout.

Lee Denton leaned against the shoulder of his leggy bay gelding and gnawed a fresh chew from a tobacco twist. Willoughby and Brubs stood between the two Ranger privates, Brubs idly scratching his butt while Willoughby clawed at the two-day stubble of beard that prickled the skin of his neck.

Dave wondered why everyone else looked so calm and loose. His own gut had knotted up like a cheap rope.

"You boys were right," Jamison said with a nod to Brubs and Willoughby. "It is Delgado's bunch. Camped for the night about eight miles above Hangtree Pass. Casey slipped in close enough to their camp last night to count the hairs in Delgado's nose holes."

"Any sign they know we're here, Casey?" Denton asked. Sinclair shook his head, scratched a match in cupped hands and fired his cigarette. "Good. That should give us an edge."

"We'll need all the edge we can get, Lee," Jamison said, his tone flat. "Casey says another three men rode into Delgado's camp just before sundown."

Denton's brow furrowed. "That doesn't help the odds much. Fifteen to three could make it a little sticky."

"Fifteen to five ain't so bad," Brubs said, "when it's just fifteen Mexes against five Texans." He flashed a grin at Willoughby. "Better make that four and a half. Dave here's tryin', but he just ain't got the hang of bein' Texan yet."

"Shut up, McCallan," Jamison said quietly.

Brubs shut.

The sergeant squatted silently for a few moments, his brow wrinkled in thought, then he picked up a mesquite twig and scratched a few lines in the sandy soil. He glared at Brubs and Willoughby. "You boys know the Chinitis?"

Willoughby shook his head. "No, sir. We've been into Mexico a couple of times, but not through that range."

Jamison sighed. "If I had any sense, I'd leave you two necked to a cactus and out of the way somewhere. Maybe I'll live to regret it, but I want Delgado, and I'll need every gun available to get him. And that means you two."

Willoughby nodded silently.

Jamison waved them closer. "Gather around,

173

then, and pay attention, because I'm only going over this once." He traced the twig over the map in the sand. "Hangtree Pass is shaped something like an hourglass. The pass flares out in a sort of meadow or valley to the north, funnels down as it cuts through the Chinitis, then opens up again this side of the Rio Grande. Got that?"

At Willoughby's nod, Jamison scratched a circle in the sand a short distance from the narrow pass. "This is the only good water and grass in the pass, and it's twenty miles to the next water hole. Delgado will likely camp there." He glanced at Sinclair. "Casey says Delgado only puts one guard on the remuda at night." He tapped the twig against his palm in thought. "We've got to hit Delgado, and hit him hard, while he's still in camp. Preferably at daybreak."

"Are you going to try to arrest him, Sergeant?"

"I'm going to ambush the bastard first, Willoughby," Jamison said, his tone as cold as the almost colorless eyes. "Then I'll explain to the corpse that it is under arrest. If I have time. This is a military operation. The idea here is assassination, raid, and retreat, not apprehension. Clear enough?"

"Yes, sir. Quite clear."

"We have two primary objectives," Jamison said. "One is to do away with Delgado. The other is to recover the stolen horses." He glanced at Sinclair. "Casey, I want you to take care of the guard and stampede the horses. The rest of us will sit tight until you're free of the field of fire."

Sinclair merely nodded.

Jamison turned back to his sketch in the sand. "Lee, you're our best hand with a rifle. I want you here." He touched the twig to the west ridge of the valley. "The rocks will give you cover. You'll have a good field of fire, but you may have to cope with the sun in your eyes."

Denton said, "No problem, boss."

"I'll take the east point, here. That will give us a good cross fire." Jamison squinted up at Willoughby and Brubs. "Willoughby, I want you and McCallan here." He touched the twig to the sand. "The canyon walls are steep, almost straight up, in that part of the pass. This is the only trail out of Hangtree to the east. Sinclair will stampede the horses along this trail. Your job is to cover him — and the other two of us — in case we have to make a run for it."

"By God, Sergeant," Brubs blurted, "that's a right good plan. I reckon ol' General Bobby Lee'd be mighty proud of you, was he here."

"I doubt that, McCallan." Jamison's tone went even colder. "I was on the other side."

"Oh," Brubs said. "You don't talk like a Yankee, the way Dave here does —"

"McCallan," Jamison pointed the twig at Brubs, "I'm beginning to get irritated with your constant jabbering. From this point onward, whenever I want a squawk from you I will yank your tail feathers. *¿Sabe?*"

"*Si, Capitán,*" Brubs said. "Just gimme my guns back and you won't hear another peep from this rooster."

"You get your guns back tomorrow morning, not before. I'll trust you when I have to and maybe not even then. And, McCallan, I will make you a sincere promise. If either of you point those weapons at anyone except a Mexican, I will personally castrate you and make you eat your own testicles. Any questions?"

Brubs shook his head emphatically. "Reckon you done explained that plain enough."

Jamison sighed. "All right, we'll change horses now and get back in the saddle. We'll be into the Cuesta del Burro range by moonrise and within two miles of Hangtree Pass by two in the morning. Then we catch fresh horses, picket the spare animals here" — he touched the twig to a point behind the east ridge — "and be in position an hour before sunrise. It will be Casey's decision when to start the fiddle. Nobody fires a shot until he's clear of camp with the horses. Men, we aren't likely to get another chance at Delgado. Let's make this one count."

The men nodded silently. "By the way, McCallan," Jamison said as he stabbed the twig into the sand, "this is the location of the famous Hangtree. If either of you screw up this operation, it would be my pleasure to show you just how effective this particular tree performs its designated duty. Is that perfectly clear?"

Willoughby felt a scratching around his neck that was not entirely due to the itchy beard stubble.

"Couldn't be no clearer," Brubs said. "Like Lee here says, you're the boss."

Jamison stood and flexed his shoulders. "All right, change horses and we'll move out. Save your best and fastest horses for tomorrow morning —" He abruptly raised a hand. "Horse coming."

Willoughby cocked his head to one side, listening. He heard nothing except the creak of saddle leather as Casey Sinclair vaulted back into the saddle and kneed the brown into motion.

"You gonna give us our guns, Jamison?" Brubs asked.

Jamison shook his head. "Not now. There's only one horse. Casey can handle it."

The dark-skinned Ranger rode back a few minutes later, leading the coyote dun, a heavy Mexican saddle on its back.

"Damn me if that horse ain't like a bad penny," Brubs muttered.

Jamison lifted an eyebrow at him. "Is this your horse, McCallan?"

Brubs shook his head. "Wouldn't have that sorry crow bait myself. That's Willoughby's horse. Was with the remuda Delgado's bunch took."

Willoughby went to the coyote dun and examined the animal. The cream-colored hide bore fresh welts from spur rowels. "It appears," Willoughby said, "that one of Delgado's men decided to try to ride him. Most likely Malhumorado bucked him off somewhere."

177

Brubs snorted. "No damn Mexican can ride that horse, he decides to pitch. If I can't ride him, nobody can."

Willoughby reached for the reins, patted the coyote dun on the neck, and started stripping the Mexican saddle from the horse's back. "I'm glad to see him, Brubs. I thought I'd lost him for sure this time."

"When you two get through yammering," Jamison said, "get your saddles on some fresh mounts. We're moving out." He studied the coyote dun for a moment. "Willoughby," Jamison said with a shake of the head, "I'm glad you got your horse back, even if he is as ugly as a vulture on a mud fence. But if we're lucky, he crippled up a bandit somewhere."

A few minutes later, Willoughby pulled the cinch tight on Choctaw. The coyote dun, haltered and on loose lead, nuzzled the flank of Willoughby's black.

"Thought Jamison said save your best horse," Brubs said as he swung his saddle onto the little gray mustang.

"I plan to ride Malhumorado tomorrow."

Brubs snorted in disdain. "That sorry plug? Hell, he's liable to poot your butt off and get you killed sure."

Willoughby forced a weak grin. "He's never even humped his back with me, Brubs. The fact that he bucks you off every time you step in the saddle just shows his good taste in riders. And as to getting me killed, you've been trying longer than he has and you haven't managed it yet."

Brubs snugged the cinch tight and swung aboard Mouse. "Don't know where you got this idea I been tryin' to get you killed, but after tomorrow it might not matter much."

Willoughby toed the stirrup. "Why do you say that?"

"On account of Delgado's men just might send us both to that big saloon in the sky."

Willoughby sighed as he swung into the saddle. "You are a true comfort to a man, Brubs McCallan."

Dave Willoughby crouched behind a notch in a jumble of boulders at the base of the narrow trail leading out of Hangtree Pass, the receiver of his Winchester slick to the touch despite the night chill that lingered in the still dawn air.

He had to admit he was still a bit frazzled from the passage through the Cuesta del Burro range. He figured his saddle horn was about the size of a Mexican bean now, as hard as he had been squeezing it. The switchback trail leading up the mountains had been barely big enough for the horses to move through single file, and in several places his right leg brushed the mountain wall and his left stirrup hung over nothing but two hundred feet of thin air. There was just enough light from the pale moon to leave a man with a serious case of the yips, watching Choctaw thread his way gingerly along the sheer mountain face. Willoughby had almost wet his drawers once when the dun's front foot slipped on a round stone; for an instant it seemed the gelding teetered over thin air before he regained his balance and scrambled on up the narrow trail.

Brubs hadn't seemed the least bit concerned during the climb up one side of the Cuesta del Burros and down the other. His little gray mustang was as surefooted as a mountain goat. Mouse hadn't even dislodged a single stone. Brubs squatted beside a juniper bush twenty feet to Willoughby's right on the far side of the pass, the old Henry cradled in the crook of an elbow. He was humming softly. Willoughby thought the tune was "Lorena," one of the favorite songs on both sides during the war — but with Brubs McCallan, it was hard to tell. He carried a tune about as well as an armadillo played a mouth harp.

Their two fresh horses, Willoughby's coyote dun and Brubs's big sorrel, Squirrel, stood behind a stand of junipers a few feet behind Willoughby's post.

Willoughby shook his head in disbelief at his partner's nerve. Less than two hours ago the scruffy little Texan had almost given Ranger Sergeant Tobin Jamison apoplexy. Jamison had, with some reluctance, returned the rifles and handguns to Brubs and Willoughby. Brubs looked at the Henry, then at Jamison, and shook his head.

"Ain't gonna fight unless you unarrest us and swear us in as Rangers," he had said.

180

Even in the darkness Willoughby thought he saw Jamison's neck flush. "What the hell are you talking about, McCallan? I'd sooner swear in a pair of Kwahadi Comanches as you two."

"Rangers get paid a dollar and a quarter a day," Brubs said pleasantly. "Dave and me need the money. We're so broke we couldn't buy a beer if whiskey was a dime a barrel."

Jamison sputtered in rage, the first time Willoughby had seen the sergeant lose his composure. But finally, he said, "All right, dammit. But only because we may need your guns. You're Rangers. I'll give you the oath when this is all over."

"Got any spare badges?" Brubs said. "Always wanted to wear one of them things."

Jamison leveled a hard, cold glare at Brubs. "Don't push me, McCallan."

Brubs said, "Just askin'. Don't go givin' yourself the vapors, Jamison." He racked the action of the Henry to chamber a cartridge, then grinned. "Don't you worry about me and Willoughby none," he said. "We'll be there when the shootin' starts."

And that, Willoughby thought, should be soon now. He wiped his sweaty palm on his pant leg and studied the valley below as the near blackness of the starlight began to give way to the coming dawn. Gilbert Delgado's camp was beginning to stir.

The bandits were camped in a grassy clearing beside a shallow creek, little more than two hun-

181

dred yards from Willoughby's vantage point near the base of the mountain trail. Mesquite, catclaw, and ocotillo cactus clumps flanked the clearing on the south and west. A smattering of cotton-woods, obviously old trees twisted by wind and some scarred by lightning, started a few yards north of the campsite and followed the winding creek. Willoughby could barely make out the faint dark shapes of the horse herd in the meadow above the cottonwoods. There seemed to be more than forty horses in the remuda. Willoughby saw only one mounted man circling the herd. He seemed to be slumped in the saddle, perhaps dozing away his turn as nighthawk.

Willoughby turned his attention back to the camp. A half dozen saddled horses stood along a picket line a few yards north of the camp. Night horses, Willoughby figured, kept saddled and handy in case of attack or a stampede by the stolen remuda.

One man, a stocky bandit wearing a sombrero the size of a saddle blanket, squatted on his heels and tossed dry sticks onto the blackened ash pile that obviously had been last night's cooking fire. Others filtered singly and in pairs into the mesquite or cactus, answering nature's call. Some still lay beneath their blankets. Willoughby counted fourteen men in the bandit camp, but from this distance and the unsure light he couldn't make out which one was Gilbert Delgado.

Willoughby flinched as the coyote dun snorted

and stomped a front foot. The noise seemed loud as a cannon shot to him, but went unheard in the camp below. The dawn light grow steadily stronger until it bathed the valley in a flat gray that cast no shadows. There was no glare. It was a good shooting light. Willoughby didn't see that as especially reassuring. Good shooting light for Rangers also was good shooting light for Mexican bandits.

Willoughby glanced again at Brubs. The stocky Texan lifted the ancient Henry from the crook of his elbow, laid the fore stock into the notch of a forked stick he had rigged as a shooting rest, and nodded toward the north end of the valley.

"Get set, partner," Brubs called in little more than a whisper, "looks like the dance is about to start."

Willoughby stared toward the upper end of the meadow and felt his heart kick into a high lope. The dozing nighthawk passed by a dense tangle of mesquite. The loop of a lariat snaked out and closed around the bandit's neck. The Mexican only had time to reach a hand toward his throat before he was yanked from the saddle. Casey Sinclair was on him before the bandit hit the ground. Light flashed against steel; the Mexican stiffened, struggled for a moment, and then went limp. Seconds later Sinclair emerged from the thicket, spurring his brown toward the horse remuda.

"Ball's open, Dave," Brubs said. "Pick your partner and fling some lead soon as Sinclair's in the clear." He nestled his cheek against the stock of the Henry.

Willoughby spent a second double-checking that a cartridge was chambered in his Winchester, then lifted the weapon to his shoulder. The distance to the camp was pushing the accuracy range of the .44-40; from here, Willoughby figured, Brubs's .44 rimfire wouldn't do much except make noise. Willoughby tensed and waited, his heart hammering against his ribs.

A shout sounded from the camp. At the edge of his vision Willoughby saw Casey Sinclair charge into the far side of the remuda, muzzle flashes from his pistol ripping into the gray dawn. The sound of the handgun shots reached Willoughby a second or so later, followed by the low thunder of horses' hooves as the animals panicked. They were at full speed within two jumps, charging toward the trail where Willoughby and Brubs waited.

The bandits stood frozen for an instant in surprise and confusion. The scant seconds were all that Sinclair needed to ride clear of the field of fire of the men on the ridge. Then one of the Mexicans dropped to a knee and whipped a rifle to his shoulder. Willoughby elevated the muzzle of his .44-40 and squeezed the trigger. The slug fell short, but hit close enough to kick sand at the bandit's knee. The rifleman's shot went wild as he flinched, glanced toward the ridge, and then dove for cover behind a pile of packs.

One man in the camp threw out his arms and

sprawled on his back; another grabbed at his hip and went down as the whip crack of big-bore rifle blasts rattled the dawn. The direction of the shots told Willoughby that Jamison and Lee Denton were in position. Willoughby slapped a quick, unaimed shot toward the camp, hit nothing but sand, and racked a fresh round into the Winchester.

Yells and yelps sounded from the camp, a half dozen voices yapping in rapid-fire Mexican. Four men sprinted toward the saddled horses waiting at the picket line. Willoughby calculated the lead, swung the muzzle of his rifle ahead of one of the running men, and squeezed the trigger. The bandit dove, then clambered to his feet and sprinted to the horses before Willoughby could fire again. Brubs's .44 rimfire popped, but the slugs fell well short of the picket line.

Willoughby flinched as a slug slapped into the rock near his head, peppering his cheek with stone shards. Through the haze of powder smoke he saw the bandits scramble for the cover of the mesquite and ocotillo; one of the fleeing men went down, flopped like a beheaded rooster, and lay still. Lee Denton and Tobin Jamison were pouring a heavy fire into the camp. Willoughby snapped a quickly aimed shot at a fleeing bandit as the man dove into the mesquites.

Powder smoke blossomed from a half dozen points in the cover around the campsite. Slugs buzzed overhead or keened off the boulders at Willoughby's post. Over the crackle of gunfire he heard the pounding hooves as the stampeded remuda charged toward him. He squinted through the dust and smoke; the lead horses were only a few yards away now, the rest close behind, spooked into a panicked run by Sinclair's whoops and pistol shots. Four bandits were now mounted and closing on Sinclair, handgun slugs kicking dust at the hooves of the Ranger's horse.

"Come on, Casey," Willoughby muttered as he rammed cartridges into the loading port of his Winchester, "just a few more yards —"

Sinclair almost made it.

Then his horse stumbled, staggered, and went down, thirty yards short of the rocks jumbled at the base of the trail. Sinclair kicked free of the stirrups, landed on his feet, then fell as the bay crumpled. Willoughby heard a whoop of triumph from one of the Mexicans bearing down on Sinclair. They were less than a hundred yards from the dismounted Ranger.

Willoughby barked a curse. He ripped the coyote dun's reins free and vaulted into the saddle. He tossed his Winchester to Brubs. "Cover me!" he yelled.

"I'll cover! You ride!"

Willoughby drove the spurs to the dun.

The lead horse thundered past, headed for the trail a half second after Willoughby's mount cleared the narrow opening. He kneed the dun around the edge of the remuda toward the downed Ranger. He heard the crack of the Winchester behind him and saw the lead bandit stiffen, then slump over the neck of his horse. The others were almost on Sinclair now. Willoughby yanked the Colt from his holster and thumbed two quick rounds toward the bandits. He knew the shots had missed, but the Mexicans instinctively checked their horses. Rifle slugs from Brubs's vantage point hummed past Willoughby's head; a Mexican's horse went down.

Willoughby heard the crack of a rifle slug past his ear, and a second later felt the numbing impact of a heavy blow against his left foot. He leaned over the coyote dun's neck, spurring the gelding to a flat-out run as he neared the downed Ranger. Sinclair knelt on the bare ground, trying to thumb cartridges into his empty Colt.

"Casey!" Willoughby yelled. He was only a few yards from Sinclair. The Ranger glanced up, saw Willoughby bearing down on him, and stood.

Willoughby checked the dun's speed a fraction, ignored the whistle of slugs past his ear, and clamped his legs tight against the coyote dun's sides. He jammed his pistol beneath his waistband, grabbed the saddle horn with his left hand, and leaned down on the dun's side.

Willoughby's forearm cracked into Sinclair's upraised hand; the jolt of the blow almost pulled him from the saddle. Then Sinclair's feet left the ground, and the Ranger swung up behind him. Willoughby kneed the dun into a tight turn; the pursuing bandits were within a few yards, almost close enough that he could see the color of their eyes.

Rifle and pistol slugs whined past. Willoughby glanced over his shoulder and saw a Mexican level his pistol from less than twenty feet away. He steeled himself for the bullet shock.

It never came. The bandit suddenly seemed to lift straight up out of the saddle, hang in the air for a moment, then fall heavily. Willoughby heard the crack of Brubs's .44 Henry. The other bandits yanked their horses around and spurred toward the nearest cover.

Willoughby ignored the buzz of lead, spurred the dun into a lunging climb up the first few yards of the trail, then reined to a sliding stop behind the boulders. Casey Sinclair slid from the dun's rump and crouched behind the boulder, Colt in hand. Willoughby stepped from the saddle, pulled his pistol from his waistband, and crouched beside Sinclair. The firing from both the camp and the valley rim seemed to have eased.

"You all right, Sinclair?" Willoughby gasped.

Sinclair merely nodded. He raised his pistol, fired, and grunted in satisfaction.

The echoes of gunfire gradually died away in the valley. Willoughby glanced at Brubs. "Dammit, Brubs, I told you to cover me," he snapped.

"And I told you to ride," Brubs yelped back. "You looked like a damn sack of spuds out there. You hit?"

Willoughby remembered the blow against his left foot. He looked down, afraid of what he might see. The heel of his left boot skewed slightly. There was no blood. And no pain. He glanced at the winded coyote dun. His left stirrup, a heavy Mexican-style arc made of four layers of tough bois d'arc wood, was splintered and shattered. There was no blood on the horse. Willoughby sighed in relief. The slug had hit the stirrup, deflected, whacked into his boot heel, and fell away, spent. "I'm all right," Willoughby called. "You Johnny Rebs never did learn to shoot!"

"Never got a shot at one of 'em's backside," Brubs yelled back, "and that's the only target we had to practice on where you Yanks was concerned!"

Willoughby realized his shirt was soaked with sweat and his fingers were trembling. He took a deep breath and wondered where in the hell he had found the courage to make that ride. He hadn't planned it. It had just happened. "Brubs," he called, "throw me my Winchester!"

"What for? You can't hit nothin' with it!" An instant later the rifle spun toward Willoughby. He caught it with one hand and started stuffing cartridges into the loading port. Willoughby became aware of an eerie silence over the valley. He glanced toward the camp. Two men lay huddled on the sand. Another bandit sprawled a few yards down slope from the trail, his sombrero crushed beneath his head.

The silence grew and thickened. Willoughby realized the two sides were in a standoff. The bandits couldn't mount a charge without exposing themselves to a blistering cross fire. The Rangers couldn't charge without riding into the teeth of a volley of lead. "What do we do now, Sinclair?"

Casey Sinclair's black eyes narrowed as he studied the outlaw hangout for several seconds. Then he shrugged.

Moments later six quick shots from a handgun sounded in the distance. Sinclair sighed, then motioned for Brubs and Willoughby to retreat up the trail to the top of the valley ridge.

Willoughby mounted, awkwardly because of the shattered stirrup, and waited for Sinclair to climb aboard behind the cantle of his saddle. Brubs sheathed his Henry and swung aboard Squirrel.

"Ready, partner?" Brubs said.

"Might as well." Willoughby touched spurs to the coyote dun.

A few rifle slugs pinged off rocks or thudded into juniper bushes as they rode, but none came close. Moments later Willoughby eased the dun to a stop beyond the ridge. Brubs reined in at his side.

"Been wonderin' somethin', partner," Brubs said casually. "Where'd you learn that pickup? Seen cavalry boys do it, but never no artillery man."

Willoughby said, "Even artillery gunners have some spare time to read the training manuals of other branches. And I saw the Comanches, the best horsemen I have ever observed, use a similar maneuver just the other day. As a favorite author of mine once wrote, 'The bookful blockhead, ignorantly read, with loads of learned lumber in his head.' "

"Say what?"

" 'Who to a friend his faults can freely show,' " Sinclair said. His voice was a surprisingly deep baritone. " 'And gladly praise the merit of a foe?' "

Willoughby's brows went up. "You know Alexander Pope?"

"Required reading at the University of Virginia. By the way, I'm in your debt. They had me cold out there." Sinclair offered a hand.

Brubs shook his head sadly. "Damn. I liked him better when he didn't talk. Now I got two book-smart college boys to fret over."

A twinkle of amusement glinted in Sinclair's deep black eyes. " 'To endeavor to work upon the vulgar with fine sense,' " he said with a nod toward Brubs, " 'is like attempting to hew blocks with a razor.' Do you suppose Pope had McCallan in mind when he wrote that?"

Willoughby said, "It wouldn't surprise me. Maybe he rode with a McCallan once."

Brubs snorted in disgust. "When you two get done quotin' verse and sippin' tea, you might give me some sort of idea what we do next." He glanced at the back trail. "I wouldn't want to get caught spoutin' poetry while a bunch of mad Mexicans is a-chousin' me."

"They won't," Sinclair said calmly. "They

191

don't have that many horses. We got away with most of their cavvy in addition to the ones they had stolen. We'll wait. Sergeant Jamison will be along soon."

Brubs frowned at the swarthy Sinclair. "I reckon you was a Yankee, too?"

Sinclair shook his head. "Fourth Georgia."

"Now, that," Brubs said with a sigh, "is a comfort to know. There for a minute I thought I was hemmed in by more Yankees than was at Chickamauga."

Tobin Jamison and Lee Denton rode up a few minutes later. "You boys okay?" Jamison asked. At their answering nods, the sergeant sighed. "Well, we got at least one of the objectives accomplished," he said. "We got the horses back and bloodied Delgado's bunch some."

"You nail that damn pepper gut horse thief?" Brubs said.

Jamison spat in disgust. "Never got a shot at Delgado. He was in the thickets making water when the shooting started. Just my luck the jackass decides to go take a leak right at that particular time. I'll get him one of these days." Jamison paused to stare at Willoughby for a moment. "I saw what you did back there, Willoughby. That took bigger *cojones* than I figured you for."

"Sinclair needed help. I didn't do anything anyone else wouldn't have done under the same circumstances."

"I doubt that," Jamison said. "You know, I'm

still trying to remember where I know you from, Willoughby." He sighed. "It'll come to me. Anyhow, you and McCallan both did the Texas Rangers proud back there. Proud enough I won't have to show you two how Hangtree Pass's most notable landmark works." He picked up the slack in the reins. "Let's get a move on, boys. We've got some horses to gather and a long ride back to Seguin."

ELEVEN

Dave Willoughby slouched in the saddle and tried to ignore the maddening itch under the thick brownish-black whiskers on his neck and chin.

In fact, he itched all over. The hair that now fell past his collar to near shoulder length was heavy with dirt and grease, and his scalp crawled as if it harbored every species of insect known to man and a few that had not yet been discovered. Brubs had been a big help, as usual. He had spent an hour yesterday talking about the tiny bugs with big bites called "no-see-'ems" by the Indians. Willoughby had been eaten up with "no-see-'ems" ever since.

His clothes were stiff with dirt, streaked with sweat and horse slobbers, and he was reasonably sure he could smell his socks through the scuffed boots on his feet.

He had never felt so grubby in his life.

Brubs, riding at his right, looked even scruffier. But then, Willoughby thought, that was Brubs's normal state of attire. Brubs could manage to look trail-worn even when he was fresh from the bathhouse and barbershop and wearing brand-new clothes still wrinkled from the store shelf.

The dust raised by the remuda wasn't helping. It sifted through the bandanna pulled over Willoughby's mouth and nose, clogged his air passages, and turned into tiny tracks of mud where it settled into sweat-soaked creases of his shirt. His once-black hat was now dust-gray, stained dark around the sweatband, its brim beginning to droop from exposure to wind and weather.

Willoughby and Brubs were riding drag again. Sergeant Tobin Jamison had the point, out where the air was relatively free of dust. Casey Sinclair rode one flank and Lee Denton the other, both horsemen at times almost obscured by the dust cloud raised by the remuda.

The drive from Hangtree Pass seemed to have taken forever, but Willoughby knew misery tended to warp a man's concept of time just as rain warped the boards of a house. The four riders had recovered all but two of the horses stolen at Seguin, along with seventeen Mexican mounts from Gilbert Delgado's outlaw band.

Brubs had found the latter acquisition quite amusing. "Bet old Delgado squalls like a goosed panther," Brubs had said, "when he figures out we done stole more horses from him than he stole from us."

The first couple of days had been hard on the nerves, constantly watching the back trail and riding with one hand on a rifle stock. But there had been no sign of pursuit. Delgado and his men, all but a few of them left afoot, made no attempt to follow. Delgado's bunch was probably in Mexico by now, licking their wounds and swilling tequila in a cool cantina, Willoughby figured. Once the initial worry over the possibility of attack by the bandits had passed, the days settled into a grinding routine that gave a man plenty of time to dwell on his own miseries.

The only thing that had helped take Willoughby's mind off his woes was the nights when he and Casey Sinclair sat by the fire and debated the philosophy of Plato and Homer and discussed the impact of early European monarchies on world history. Around the other men Sinclair was just as closemouthed and reticent as ever. It was, Willoughby mused, as though the swarthy Ranger was somehow ashamed of his education. Or maybe he simply chose not to flaunt it, thinking that might be seen as boasting by his saddle mates or somehow tarnish his reputation as a tough and dangerous man. Casey Sinclair, Willoughby decided, was a puzzle wrapped in an enigma inside a locked box.

Brubs interrupted Willoughby's musings. "Say, partner," he said, "how's about letting me ride on your upwind side? You're gettin' ripe as a trail drive cowpuncher two months out of Texas and a week short of Dodge. Smellin' more like a real Texan every day."

Willoughby swatted at a sand fly boring into his neck and said, "It never ceases to amaze me, Brubs McCallan, how you find so much delight in another man's miseries." His voice was slightly muffled from the dirty bandanna around his face. "If we get out of this mess without getting hanged, I am going to spend about three weeks soaking in a hot tub and shaving every hour and a half."

Willoughby wondered how Brubs kept the dust out of his teeth when he grinned all the time. "Amigo," Brubs said, "you are now gettin' a taste of what life was like in the Army of the Confederacy. Except that now we got boots on our feet and grub in our bellies."

Irritation flared in Willoughby's cheeks. "It wasn't exactly a bed of roses for the Union Army, as I recall it."

"Reckon you're right at that, partner," Brubs said solemnly. "Wasn't just fightin' the other side made that little fracas such a pain in the butt. Never got so tired of mud and bugs in my whole life, and I been in a bunch of each many a time. Reckon it's like General Bobby Lee said. They never was a good war or a bad peace."

Willoughby thought for a moment about correcting Brubs's history, then decided it didn't matter a whit if Benjamin Franklin got proper credit for the quote or not. Who said it didn't change the truth of the statement.

The two rode in silence for a few minutes. Willoughby pulled the bandanna down, snorted dust from his nostrils, and wiped a grimy hand across his sweaty forehead. The pensive look faded from Brubs's sun-browned face. He reined closer, reached out, and clapped Willoughby on the shoulder. "Don't work yourself into a snit, partner. We'll be in Seguin in a couple of days and it'll all be done with. And I know these two gals —"

"Brubs," Willoughby said, "I am not interested

at the moment in your two girls. I can't share your optimism that we are going to get out of this without a rope around our necks. Suppose that clerk recognizes us? What if Lawrence T. Pettibone shows up?"

The grin faded from Brubs's face. "No call to fret about that four-eyed bank clerk. We done got it worked out how we're gonna get past him. As to old man Pettibone, we just got to trust our guardian angel to keep him too busy countin' his money or foreclosin' on another poor rancher to show up in Seguin." He shifted his weight in the saddle. "But now you mention it, somethin' has been gnawin' at me," he said. "Jamison's been lookin' at you funny-like the last few days. Could be he's just about to figure out how come you look familiar. You sure you didn't run across him somewheres?"

Willoughby said, "I cannot, for the life of me, remember ever having seen that man before he showed up on our trail."

"Maybe he just thinks he knows you," Brubs said with a shrug. "Mighta mistook you for some town dandy somewhere. You wasn't runnin' from the law when you started that saloon fight down in San 'Tone, was you?"

Willoughby glared at him. "In the first place, *I* didn't start the fight. In the second place, I was never in a minute's trouble with the law or anyone else until I met you. However, in that short span of less than a year, I have progressed from being honest but poor to being dishonest and poor." He sighed heavily. "I suppose that, in your peculiar way of looking at the foibles of man and life, is character development of the first magnitude."

Brubs clapped him on the shoulder again. "You come a long ways toward bein' a real genuine Texan at that, Dave. You'll do to ride the river with." He chuckled aloud. "We have had us some fun, ain't we? And we got a bunch more waitin' for us. Them two girls at Seguin, for starters —"

Willoughby said, *"Vitae summa brevis spem nos vetat incohare longam."*

"Talk American."

"Horace wrote that. It says, 'Life's short span forbids us to enter on far-reaching hopes.' "

Brubs's brow wrinkled in thought. "Maybe this Horace feller had ahold of the pot handle after all. Makes sense when you study on it. Life's plumb short enough, that's a pure fact." The frown faded. "But partner, we don't have to reach far to slap a little hope on them two gals. Now, I ain't sayin' one of 'em ain't maybe a touch on the homely side. Mabel, she's sort of got a mule nose on her and she's maybe a tad flat up front, and if you don't look close at that hairy wart on her chin it don't look too bad. I reckon you'll like her. Now, Jessica — that's Mabel's cousin — I tell you, the way she's put together'll make a man's neck get stud hoss thick and have him pawin' the ground and snortin' loud."

Willoughby quit listening. When Brubs McCallan started talking about women, he could go on for hours.

He did.

Brubs had worked his way back through the history of Texas femininity to his first true love, Susie Poindexter of the Nacogdoches Poindexters, and the hayloft in the barn behind the school, before Jamison called a halt for the night.

It was Lee Denton's turn at the cook fire. Give Jamison credit for being a quick learner, Willoughby thought; one day with Brubs on the business end of the skillet had been enough. Jamison hadn't outright criticized Brubs's cooking, but only because that was an unspoken rule in trail camps. Never criticize the cook even if you weren't sure what the lumps in the gravy were. He might tell you.

Willoughby sagged onto his bedroll after tending to the horses and scrubbing his eating utensils as clean as possible without hot water. He was tired to the bone. His spirits weren't helped much when Jamison dispatched Sinclair to take the first shift nighthawking the remuda. There would be no discussion of history and philosophy tonight. Denton had the second watch and Jamison the third.

Jamison perched cross-legged on his bedroll, coffee cup in hand, and stared hard at Willoughby. The look in the blue eyes was enough to curdle a man's blood.

"I almost had you pegged a minute ago, Willoughby," Jamison said. "It really bothers me when there's something about a man I should know and can't come up with. I *know* I've seen you somewhere." Jamison shrugged, tossed out the dregs of his coffee, and spread his blankets. "It will come to me, in time."

It seemed to Willoughby that he could feel the Ranger sergeant's stare even after Jamison pulled his hat down over his eyes and started snoring softly. Willoughby was still fretting about it when sleep finally came.

Brubs sat ramrod straight in the saddle, whistling at, over, and around "Somebody's Darling," which wasn't doing Dave Willoughby's nerves that much good.

The fact that he was whistling it while riding along the main street of Seguin behind a herd of stolen horses wasn't helping, either. And for that matter, Willoughby grumbled to himself, Brubs didn't even look like Brubs.

McCallan was clean-shaven. He had almost wrecked Willoughby's razor in the process. His bushy sand-colored handlebar mustache was neatly trimmed and his hair was cut short. Willoughby doubted the shears in Sergeant Jamison's field kit would ever recover. Brubs had used up the last slivers of Willoughby's remaining soap and borrowed Dave's only clean shirt. The shirt was snug across the shoulders, and even with the sleeves turned up several rolls they were still too long for Brubs's badger-like arms. He had even swiped a wet cloth across his boots for the first time since he had pulled them off the store shelves. He brushed most of the dust from his hat and put a semblance of shape back in it during the water stop at the stream a couple of miles outside of town.

Brubs McCallan looked only slightly scruffy. It was totally out of character.

Willoughby himself felt like the floor of a stall in a stable that hadn't been cleaned for months. Even the black gelding had fluttered its nostrils when Willoughby saddled up this morning. He couldn't be sure whether the horse was just blowing snot or snorting away the Willoughby smell.

Ranger Sergeant Tobin Jamison reined his horse in at the hitch rail in front of the bank and waved for Lee Denton, riding point, to hold up the remuda. He walked into the bank and came out a few minutes later with the clerk and a skinny man wearing a bowler hat and an expensive silk suit trailing behind.

Willoughby slouched deeper in the saddle and waited for the finger of doom to stab his way. He felt a prickle along his neck that wasn't altogether because of the whiskers. The bank clerk wiped his spectacles with a handkerchief, then squinted at each of the men with the stolen horse herd.

The clerk turned, said something to the sergeant, then shook his head. Willoughby couldn't make out the words, but he felt a flood of relief at the head shake. Apparently the old man hadn't recognized either of them. Jamison shrugged as if it didn't matter one way or the other, then spoke quietly for a few moments with the man in the silk suit.

Jamison stopped from the bank's porch. "Casey, you and the other boys take these horses back to the Bar F. Put them in the holding pasture north of the house." He nodded toward the aging clerk. "Mr. Ransom here will be along shortly to make a final tally of the horses." The cold blue gaze settled briefly on Willoughby. "I have some business here in town. I'll be at the ranch in an hour or so."

Sinclair nodded and moved up to take the point.

Willoughby felt Jamison's stare, an icy spot between his shoulder blades, as he kneed the black into motion. At Willoughby's left, Brubs tipped his hat to a pretty young girl standing on the boardwalk in front of a bakery shop. "Good mornin', miss," Brubs said. "Beautiful day sure 'nuff, ain't it?"

Willoughby couldn't relax even when Seguin had dropped a mile behind.

"What's eatin' you, partner?" Brubs said after a time. "We got her made now. I told you that four-eyed bank clerk couldn't of knowed his own ma. Relax. You're all wound up like one of them eight-day clocks."

"I will relax," Willoughby said grimly, "when we are about two hundred miles away from Seguin, three Texas Rangers, and one Lawrence

T. Pettibone. Not a moment before."

"Shoot, partner, we know Pettibone ain't around."

"And just how do we knew that?"

Brubs chuckled. "Nobody shot us, did they?"

"Not yet, anyway."

Brubs rode for a moment in silence, then sighed. "Know what frosts my drawers, partner?"

"What?"

"I done went and got all gussied up for nothin'." Brubs leaned over and spat. "Now I got to do it all again for Jessica. And it ain't nowhere near September yet."

Jamison reached the Bar F as bank clerk Ransom completed the final count of the horses. Brubs and Willoughby leaned against the rail fence a few yards from the clerk, trying to look as relaxed and inconspicuous as possible. There was, Willoughby had pointed out, no need to take a chance that Ransom might yet recognize them. He had also reminded Brubs not to do any talking within the range of Ransom's hearing. The old man might recognize his voice.

Ransom tucked a stub of a pencil into a vest pocket and nodded to the Ranger. "All the bank's horses are here except for two, Sergeant. Where did the other animals come from?"

Jamison said, "We picked up some strays along the way. If you don't mind keeping them here for a few days, we'll see if we can find out who they belong to."

"That's no problem. We have plenty of water

and grass here." Ransom nodded toward the house. "Would you men like some coffee? Or maybe something stronger?"

Jamison shook his head. "Thanks for the offer, but we have to move on." He glanced at Sinclair and Denton as the clerk strode away toward the house. "Sorry, boys, but it's back in the saddle for us. Orders were waiting at the sheriff's office. We're being sent to DeWitt County. The Sutton-Taylor feud's broken out again."

Denton shook his head in disgust. Sinclair merely frowned and nodded.

Jamison leveled a hard stare at Willoughby and McCallan. "You boys are free to go," he said. Willoughby thought the Ranger sounded disappointed. "I've no further reason to hold you."

Willoughby's gut untied itself for the first time in days. He loosed a deep sigh of relief and reached for the black's reins.

"Before you go," Jamison said, "I have something for you two." He reached in a shirt pocket, produced a roll of money, and thumbed out a few bills. "The Seguin Bank and Trust posted a reward for return of· the horses. I suppose you two should share in the money. It comes to thirty-five dollars each." He handed the bills to Brubs.

"Well, I'll be damned," Brubs said, "A whole thirty-five apiece for bringin' back a thousand dollars' worth of horses. Don't the generosity of these bankers just warm your cockles?" He tucked the money into a shirt pocket and lifted

205

an eyebrow at Jamison. "Don't we have some Rangerin' money comin' too, Sergeant?"

"Forget it, Brubs," Willoughby said. "Let's go."

"Now, hold up a minute, Dave. We earned that money. Rangerin's a right tough game."

Jamison glowered at Brubs for a long moment, then shrugged. "I suppose you did earn it, at that. One day's pay, a dollar and a quarter each —"

"One day!" Brubs squawked. "Way I figure it, we got six days' pay comin'. One day at Hangtree, five more trailin' these broomtails back here."

"McCallan," Jamison said, his tone cold, "you are some piece of work. Our agreement was I'd swear you in to help get the horses back."

Brubs nodded. "And you think back on it, Jamison, you didn't never unswear us. That makes six days."

Jamison's stare went even colder. "All right. The Texas Rangers pay their debts, even if they are somewhat questionable." He pulled the bills from his pocket, counted out fifteen dollars, and handed it to Brubs. "It might be worth it just to get you out of my hair."

Brubs thumbed the bills. "Say, Sergeant, you got any change? Hard to split three fives two ways."

"Don't push your luck, McCallan." Jamison's voice was soft, but the words had a cutting edge to them.

Brubs said, "Just thought I'd ask." He tucked the money into his pocket and turned to Willoughby. "Let's go, partner. We done our law and order duty, and them two girls is waitin' —"

"Hold up a minute," Jamison barked. He stared hard at Dave. "Now I remember who you are, Willoughby."

Willoughby's blood went cold. They had been so close to riding out, free and clear. He tried to ignore the sudden convulsion in his gut. He had to work his jaw twice to get the words out. "I still don't recall our having met, Sergeant."

"We haven't. At least not face-to-face. I was corporal of the color guard that day, the final troop muster on the parade ground at Appomattox." The ice melted from Jamison's gaze. "I was about twenty feet away when General Ulysses S. Grant himself pinned the medal on you." He thrust out a hand. "I've never had the pleasure of personally meeting a Congressional Medal of Honor winner, Lieutenant Willoughby."

Dave let his breath out in a deep sigh of relief. He took Jamison's hand.

"Medal of Honor? Willoughby?" Brubs sounded like he had just been told his partner had three heads.

Willoughby glanced at Brubs. "I didn't do much."

"Didn't do much?" Jamison pumped his hand. "McCallan, your partner saved his battery from being overrun at Sharpsburg and turned back a Rebel force trying to flank the Union lines. Then he ran onto the battlefield and pulled five wounded men to safety through a storm of musket fire and canister shot. I knew I had seen you somewhere before, Willoughby. I guess now I can rest easy."

"So can I, Sergeant," Willoughby said earnestly. "If you don't mind, I think we should be on our way."

Brubs rode in uncharacteristic silence for almost a mile after the two said their good-byes to the Rangers and the bank clerk. Finally, he shook his head. "Well, I'll be plucked for a Sunday pullet. A real war hero. Who would of thunk it of old Dave Willoughby?"

Willoughby shrugged, a bit embarrassed by all the attention. "Men do crazy things in the heat of battle, Brubs. I didn't plan it. It just happened. I didn't even want the damn medal because too many good men died that day. And my battery killed a lot of them."

Brubs nodded, his expression grim. "Reckon I know how you feel, partner. Got a little tired of walkin' over dead men myself. They'd left that war up to us privates, we'd of settled it in a poker game by sundown of the first day and everbody coulda went home." He fell silent for a moment, then glanced again at Willoughby. "Partner, you are just plumb full of surprises. Medal of Honor, yet. Won by a guy who gets cold sweats over facin' a few Injuns or a couple Mexicans."

"If you don't mind, Brubs," Willoughby said, "I'd just as soon drop the topic. I've been trying my best to forget that war."

Brubs said, "I know just the thing to get your mind off it, amigo. A couple of shots of good whiskey and a night with Mabel will straighten the kinks out of your thinkin' right nice."

Willoughby pulled the black to an abrupt stop and glared at him. "We are *not* going into any saloons. We are not going to drink any whiskey, and we are not going to call on Mabel and Jessica."

Brubs reined Squirrel around. "You got another one of them wasps in your drawers, partner?"

"Yes, I do. This time, I will not wake up in the morning in jail, broke, beaten up, shot at, or suffering from a hangover. In case you haven't noticed, we are not exactly overwhelmed with riches."

"There you go frettin' about money again. Always countin' pennies. We got plenty."

"We have enough to buy each of us a bath, a shave, a haircut, a new shirt, and supplies enough to see us back to LaQuesta. And a new razor. Which," Willoughby added with finality, "is all we are going to buy in Seguin."

Brubs frowned. "Now, Dave, ain't I been behavin' myself nigh on to a whole month now? I ain't had a drop of whiskey and I sure ain't had no women."

Willoughby said, "Only because there was neither available out in the middle of nowhere."

"Don't matter. It's still downright un-Texan,

a man goin' that long with nothin' to cut the trail dust." Brubs's frown dissolved into the beginnings of a smile. "Whiskey ain't but a couple dollars a bottle, and them girls won't cost us nothin'. Them two is how come Texas is known as the true land of the free."

"No. Every time I get mixed up with one of these women you know, I barely escape alive. And that is my final word on the matter."

Brubs's forehead wrinkled in a frown. "Dave, I plumb worry about you sometimes, frettin' over little things."

"Like husbands with ten-gauge shotguns?"

Brubs said, "Wish you coulda seen your face that time, partner. And I never seen a Yank before could outrun me, but you done it." The twinkle returned to his eyes. "I'm gonna need help with them cousins." He reined the sorrel toward town. "Be mighty sad to have Mabel's feelin's hurt, was she to get left out of all the fun. And I ain't sure I can handle her after a tumble with Jessica. That Jessica does wear a man down some."

"No way, Brubs McCallan," Willoughby growled, "and that is my final and absolute stand on the matter."

Willoughby sighed in contentment and idly stroked the long black hair of the naked woman lying beside him.

Jessica snuggled against his shoulder, a single oil lamp bathing her smooth skin in golden light.

Brubs had been right, Willoughby mused. Jessica was one fine-looking woman. Even when she had her clothes on. Which hadn't been for the last couple of hours.

"Dave?" The call from the adjoining room was only slightly muffled by the thin walls.

"What?"

"You done with my woman yet?"

Willoughby patted Jessica on the hip and lifted a questioning eyebrow. She nodded, a wisp of a smile on her full lips. "I think so," he called back. He sighed, stretched, and reached for his pants draped over the chair by the bed. The sheets rustled as Jessica pulled them up to her shoulders.

Brubs wandered in a moment later, fully dressed, hat in hand, wild sandy hair splayed in all directions like a Spanish dagger plant after a summer rain. He stared quizzically at Jessica, then shook his head. "I swear, I don't know how he does it," Brubs muttered.

"Does what?"

"Never you mind, honey," Brubs said softly. He tilted his head toward the next room. "Mabel's plumb done in. Nigh upon to wore me down, too. When she wakes up, tell her I said *gracias*. And that I sure had a fine time tonight."

"You weren't the only one," Jessica said. She slowly closed one hazel eye in a lecherous wink and nodded at Willoughby. "Feel free to drag this one in with you anytime you're in Seguin, Brubs."

Willoughby felt his cheeks redden. Back East, women were supposed to be coy and demure. Jessica wasn't the least embarrassed about speaking her mind, even if the words seemed a little crude at times. Maybe, Willoughby thought, Jessica was a female version of one of Brubs's real genuine Texans. There certainly wasn't any question about her being all woman. He buttoned his shirt and reached for his pistol belt.

"You might want to get a little more of a move on partner," Brubs said casually.

Willoughby's heart skipped a beat. He froze, his hand on the buckle of the gun belt. "Who's coming this time? Another husband?"

Brubs shrugged. "Nah. Jessica ain't wearin' no man's bit and bridle yet."

Willoughby sighed in relief. "You had me worried there for a minute. So what's the big hurry?"

Brubs idly scratched his rump. "Somethin' I sort of forgot to mention, what with my mind elsewheres the last few hours." He clapped his hat on his head and nodded to Jessica. "Hate to leave such fine company so quick, honey, but it's gettin' on toward midnight. Time for me and Dave to get to work."

Willoughby paused in the act of pulling on a boot. "Work?"

"It's a strange time to be going to work, Brubs," Jessica said. It was a question as well as a statement.

Brubs grinned. "You may have noticed old Dave here does his best work in the dark. Come on, partner. I'll tell you about it while we saddle up."

A short time later, Willoughby hefted the heavy stock saddle onto Choctaw's back, snugged the cinches, and turned to Brubs as the stocky Texan finished lashing the supply packs in place on the spare horses by the light of a single lantern. "Now, what's all this about work?"

Brubs yanked at a cross brace of a packsaddle and grunted in satisfaction. "While you was dawdlin' around wastin' our hard-earned money on soap and water and trail truck, I was cuttin' a little dust down to the saloon —"

"Get to the point, Brubs."

"I'm gettin' there, partner." Brubs sniffed. "Most unpatientest feller I ever seen. Like I was fixin' to say, while you was piddlin' around in the barbershop I was workin'. Found us a horse buyer."

"A horse buyer?"

"Feller from over in Williamson County. Needs twenty cow ponies. He'll pay twenty-five a head if we get 'em trailed to Round Rock by sundown tomorrow."

Willoughby scowled. "But, Brubs, we don't have twenty horses —" He suddenly stiffened, his eyes narrowing. "Wait a minute! You're not thinking what I think you're thinking?"

Brubs's said, "Sure am. We're ridin' back out to the Bar F."

TWELVE

Dave Willoughby pulled Choctaw to a stop in the trees behind the Bar F ranch, turned to Brubs and shook his head in disbelief. "I was right," he said. "Insanity is contagious I caught it from you."

Brubs ignored the mild barb. "We got us a fine horseborrowin' light tonight, partner. A real Comanche moon."

The full white disk overhead bathed the house, barn, and horse pasture in light that seemed bright enough to read by. Willoughby could almost make out the color of individual horses a hundred yards away.

"Comanche moon?"

Brubs shifted his weight. The creak of saddle leather sounded unusually loud in the still night air. "That's right. Nights like this, full moon durin' what the Comanch call tall grass time. That's when they make their biggest raids."

"That," Willoughby said, "is a comforting thought."

Brubs spat. "Ain't nothin' to fret over, partner. There ain't that many Comanch left nowadays. Why, just after the war, I seen raidin' parties of two, three hundred Injun bucks in one camp on a night like this." He shrugged. "Shoot, wouldn't likely be more'n thirty, forty Injuns in any war party out these days."

Willoughby sighed. "Not more than thirty or forty. That makes me feel a lot better."

The two watched the house in silence for a time. No lights showed in any of the windows.

"Looks like old man Ransom's turned in for the night," Brubs said.

"As we should have," Willoughby said. "I can't believe we're going to steal those same horses again. Not so soon after bringing them back."

"Best time to do it, amigo. Won't nobody else expect it either." He added, "Bet that silk-suit banker and old man Pettibone have walleyed fits when them horses gets gone again. Serves 'em right, takin' a poor man's place like that. Besides, I figure they stole 'em in the first place. They just done it with a piece of paper 'stead of the right and proper way. People like that gives us honest horse thieves a plumb bad name."

Willoughby twisted in the saddle to look back over the road to Seguin. "I'm not convinced this is such a good idea. I don't want that Ranger Jamison on my trail again."

"What ain't no problem. Jamison's halfway to DeWitt County by now. Want a snort?" Brubs lifted his canteen and twisted it open. Willoughby could smell the whiskey as soon as the cap cleared the neck. He shook his head and turned back to study the ranch.

"Brubs, I don't want to see that old man hurt," Willoughby said solemnly.

Brubs downed a swallow from the canteen. "We ain't gonna hurt him."

"If we simply march up and knock on the door like we did last time, he won't answer," Willoughby said. "And if he does, he just might have a shotgun in his hand."

Brubs's grin was clear in the moonlight dappling through the trees. "I got that figured out, partner. You just leave it to old Brubs." He dismounted and handed the reins to Willoughby. "I'll whistle when he's tucked in safe for the night." Brubs strode away and vanished into the night.

It seemed to Willoughby that hours had passed since Brubs left the trees, but he knew it couldn't have been more than thirty minutes before a light flared in a window of the ranch house.

Willoughby tensed and lifted himself in the stirrups as the bank clerk stepped out the back door, clad only in his nightshirt and holding a lantern at shoulder height. He shuffled to the two-holer outhouse, lifted the length of lumber that barred the door, and stepped inside.

A short, stocky figure darted from the shadows beside the outhouse, slammed the door, and dropped the bar into place. Willoughby heard the muffled squawk from inside, a pounding on the walls, then Brubs's whistle.

Brubs was leaning casually against the outhouse door when Willoughby rode up, leading Squirrel. The pounding on the door was insistent. "Let me out of here! Open the door!" The bank clerk's voice carried well through the thin walls of the two-holer.

"Can't do that, Mr. Ransom," Brubs said.

There was a moment's stunned silence from inside the outhouse. "That voice — it's you again! You're the same one who robbed me before!"

"Ain't robbin' you personal, Mr. Ransom," Brubs said. "We're just takin' a few horses from the banker and that skinflint Lawrence T. Pettibone."

A low moan sounded through the walls. "Mister, please. I'll lose my job for sure, and I got a widowed daughter and two grandkids to support!"

"You tell that turkey-necked nickel-squeezin' banker that if he fires you, we'll bust his bank and take ever' coin he's got," Brubs said, his tone sharp. "Us Clantons takes care of our friends, and you're one of 'em."

"Clantons?" The clerk's voice was even more shaky than before.

Brubs swung into the saddle. "Don't you fret none, Mr. Ransom. You'll be all right in there till somebody comes. Might be smellin' a tad ripe by mornin', but you won't have to walk near so far to take a leak."

"Please — don't leave me locked up in here!" The pounding started again.

Brubs took the slack from his bridle reins. "Mr. Ransom, was I you, I wouldn't be poundin' on them walls much more. Might stir up some of them black widder spiders lives in outhouses."

The pounding abruptly stopped.

Brubs reined his horse toward the rail-fenced horse pasture a few yards away and said to Willoughby, "See, partner? I told you we wouldn't hurt him none."

"How did you know he'd come out?"

Brubs shrugged. "Old men got weak bladders. I figure old Ransom was somethin' like you, Dave — finicky about usin' a chamber pot on account of the smell. Me, I'd have just hung her out a window and let 'er rip."

"And the warning? About us Clantons?"

Brubs said, "Layin' a little false trail. Wouldn't hurt them Clantons none to have the law pryin' into their business. Let's go gather some horses, partner. It's a long ride from here to Round Rock."

"Which ones will we take?"

"All of 'em," Brubs said.

"But Brubs, that buyer said he only needed twenty." Dave dismounted to drop the bars of the gate to the holding pasture. "What are we going to do with the extra ones?"

Brubs said, "Why, partner, you done forgot we never made it to Mexico the first time we swiped these ponies. I reckon that grandee down to Sonora's still in the horse market. Sort of be fun to sell him them horses we swiped from Delgado."

Willoughby stepped back into the saddle. "That Ranger was right, Brubs. You are a piece of work."

Brubs said, "I'll take the point. These horses is so trailbroke now they'd probably foller a billy goat. Another couple weeks, partner, we'll be back in LaQuesta, fat, happy, countin' silver and sippin' whiskey."

Willoughby couldn't help but feel a bit edgy as he trailed the stolen horses down the main street of Round Rock. It seemed to him that every man in town carried at least two pistols. Even the farmers in bib overalls and brogans had revolvers stuck in their pockets. And every one on the street looked surly.

The atmosphere didn't improve while he waited for Brubs to locate the horse buyer after they had corralled the animals in the livery corral on the northeast side of town. Passersby stopped to glare suspiciously at the man on the big roan. Willoughby tried a couple of times to nod a greeting and got only silent stares in reply. He was getting more than a little fidgety before Brubs returned.

The man with Brubs was a good four inches taller than Willoughby's six two, muscled like a lumberjack, carried a Smith & Wesson .44 in a worn holster, and had the coldest hazel eyes Willoughby had ever seen.

Brubs nodded toward the big man. "This here's Quint Anson, the horse buyer I met in Seguin. My partner, Dave Willoughby."

A flat, icy stare was Anson's only acknowledgment of Willoughby's nod of greeting. The stare was like looking into the eyes of a scorpion. Willoughby felt a distinct sense of relief when

Anson finally shifted his gaze to the remuda. The big man pulled a plug of tobacco from his pocket, bit off a chew, and settled the tobacco into his cheek. He studied the horses for several minutes in silence. Willoughby noticed that even Brubs wasn't talking.

Finally, Anson turned away from the fence and spat. "Those the best you got?" His voice sounded like the scrape of a shovel on a gravel bed.

"Yes, sir," Brubs said. "Matter of fact, right now them's all we got. Brung the whole cavvy so's you could take your pick."

Anson's eyes narrowed. "About half of those horses are pure Mexican plugs. Not worth a dime on a cow outfit." He worked the chew for a moment and spat again. "Wouldn't ride a Mexican nag myself. Wouldn't hire a man who did." He turned to study the remuda again. "Those horses look a little gaunt in the flank."

"Well, they been a few miles here lately," Brubs said. "A couple days grass and water, they'll flesh out fine."

"The ones wearing the Bar F will do," Anson said. He nodded toward the coyote dun. "That," he said, "is the ugliest damn horse I've ever seen, and I've seen a few."

"Well, sir," Brubs said, "the prettiest woman ain't always the best cook. That's a mighty fine cow pony. Old Dave here's took kind of a shine to him. Reckon we didn't much want to sell him, nohow."

"I'll take him."

Brubs said to Willoughby, "How about it, partner? You willin' to part with old Malhumorado?"

"I said I'd take him, McCallan." Anson's tone left no doubt he *would* take the coyote dun — one way or another.

Willoughby nodded silently.

"All right," Anson said, "that's nineteen head. Twenty-five apiece." He pulled a thick sheaf of bills from his pocket. "Four seventy-five total." He counted out the bills and handed them to Brubs.

"Dave'll give you a bill of sale —"

"Why the hell do I need a bill of sale?" Anson's voice held a challenge. "You think somebody's going to accuse *me* of riding a stolen horse?"

Brubs's Adam's apple bobbed. "No, sir. I don't reckon they would at that."

"A couple of my boys are at the saloon. I'll send them down to trail these broomtails to the ranch." Anson turned and strode away without another word.

Willoughby sighed in relief when the big man rounded a corner and disappeared from sight behind a building.

"That there," Brubs said, "is one hombre I sure as hell don't never plan to cross."

Willoughby nodded. "I was thinking the very same thing. Now, before you start telling me about this fine saloon and these two girls you know in Round Rock, Brubs," he said ominously, "this time I am *not* going to go along with it. If I have to belt you up beside the head and throw

221

you over the saddle, we are leaving this town. Now."

"Partner," Brubs said, "if you don't hurry up, you're gonna be a couple miles behind me. Let's get them Mexican nags separated out and hit the trail."

Willoughby's eyes went wide in surprise. "You're not going to argue with me?"

"Hell, no," Brubs said emphatically, "this place is plumb downright spooky. Big fight buildin' between the big landowners like Anson and the grange crowd. Plus, I'd just as leave not be around if Quint Anson decides to saddle up that coyote dun."

Dave Willoughby leaned back against his saddle and watched the moon inch its way down the western sky. They had covered better than twenty miles from Round Rock before Brubs called a halt to rest the horses and brew a pot of coffee.

Willoughby would have felt better if they had covered another twenty. His nerves still hadn't quit twanging, despite the peace and calm of the campsite. A coyote yipped and howled in the distance. A nighthawk prowled the moonlit sky on silent wings. Brubs squatted by the small fire and whistled softly, but this time the off-key tune didn't get under Willoughby's skin. Brubs hadn't cracked a grin since they had left Round Rock. When Brubs McCallan had the yips, any sane man should worry.

"Brubs," Willoughby finally said, "just who is this Quint Anson?"

Brubs lifted the coffeepot lid and dumped in a handful of grounds. "Guess you could say he's the meanest man in Texas," Brubs said. "Story is he's killed better'n twenty men, one of 'em over a dollar bet that didn't get paid. Shot two Mexicans off a fence rail 'cause he didn't like 'em wearin' those serapes around a herd. Man's pure poison."

Willoughby fell silent for a moment, then said, "We have to find better quality customers, Brubs. Or go into another line of work."

"Work?" Brubs's grin finally reappeared. "Like cowboyin' or some such?" He shook his head in dismay. "And miss all this? Bein' free, not tied to no clock or calendar, and not answerin' to no man? Workin' when we want and loafin' when we want? Partner, you add her all up and we got the best jobs in Texas right now."

"I was just thinking it might be easier on the nerves."

"Nerves is what a man makes 'em, Dave." Brubs lifted the coffeepot lid, added a splash of cold water to settle the grounds. He lifted an eyebrow at Willoughby. "Now, you, for instance. I reckon you could go back East. Sleep in a soft bed with clean sheets instead of sharin' some dirty blankets with all kinds of cooties and other critters. Have that sweet little thing your folks picked out for you fixin' you three hot meals a day instead of eatin' when you can and what you've got. Sip a little high-dollar wine off a lace tablecloth instead of a shot of Old Gutwrecker off a splintery pine bar." He filled two coffee cups and handed one to Willoughby. "You'd have all the money you'd ever need. And all you'd have to do is take orders every blessed day from your pa and brother, ask when it'd be all right to go to the outhouse, and —"

"Whoa up, Brubs," Willoughby said, lifting a hand. "I think you just made your point. *'Da mihi castitatem et continentiam, sed noli modo.'*"

"Talk American."

"A quote from Saint Augustine. It says, 'Give me chastity and continence — but not yet.'"

Brubs sipped at his coffee, then chuckled. "Now that there was a man knows how to live. Reckon he'd have made a passin' fair Texan. And a saint, at that." He reached for his canteen, held it to his ear, and gave it a shake. "Sounds like there's a couple of swigs of Old Headacher left in here. Want a snort?"

Willoughby reached for the canteen. "Might as well." He uncapped the canteen and held it aloft. "A toast, my grubby little friend — to our newly found patron saint."

"Patron saint?"

"Sure. Every trade has a patron saint. I propose we adopt Saint Augustine as the official patron saint of Texas horse thieves." He downed a swig of whiskey and winced. "God that stuff is downright awful. You want me to spare you the miseries and finish it off?"

Brubs snatched the canteen. "Partners suffer equal on the trail." He hoisted the canteen. "To Saint Augustine, and may he lay some sort of blessin' on us poor hardworkin' horse thieves." Brubs drained the canteen, grimaced, and wiped his lips. "You're right. That stuff'd take the hair off a grizzly, sure 'nuff. Maybe we can't find us no better quality buyers, amigo, but when we get these nags sold in Mexico we can sure 'nuff afford us some better drinkin' whiskey."

The shot of liquor left a warm glow in Willoughby's belly. He added a swallow of strong black coffee to the coals in his gut and sighed, finally able to enjoy the serene peace of the camp. After a few minutes he rose, refilled his cup, and squatted by the fire. "Brubs?"

"Yeah?"

"How did you know I was thinking about keeping the coyote dun for myself?"

Brubs clucked his tongue. "Man gets to where he can read the way his friends look at horses and women. You was lookin' at that coyote dun sort of calf-eyed." He shook his head. "Partner, we just flat out can't keep that sorry-lookin' plug."

"Why not?"

Brubs said, "How many times we stole and sold that boss?"

Willoughby thought for a moment. "Well, let's see. I've lost track of how many times we've stolen him. But we've sold him three times, I suppose."

"And Bass Jernigan said he'd sold him twice. That was before he bought him from us down in Goliad. See what I mean, amigo? Ever'body in the horse business is flat makin' a fortune off that broomtail. We can't *afford to* keep him. It'd cause one of them financial panics all across Texas." Brubs spread his bedroll. "Better rest while you can. We'll be movin' out at first light."

Willoughby finished his coffee and spread his own blankets. He was just about to drift off when Brubs broke the silence.

"Dave?"

"Hmph?"

"Back there in Seguin, you done it to me again."

"Did what?"

"I do all the work, all the sweet talkin', and you get the smoothest honey."

"What in hell are you talking about, Brubs?"

"Jessica. I can't for the life of me figure out how come you always get the best-lookin' filly when it's me rounds up the remuda."

Willoughby couldn't help but grin. "I don't know," he said. "Unlucky at cards, lucky at love, I guess."

"May be somethin' to that. You sure as hell can't play poker," Brubs said. "Reckon it worked out okay, though. That Mabel maybe ain't such a looker, but I don't reckon I ever had better."

Willoughby said, "Brubs, what was the best you ever had?"

Brubs said, "The last and the next." He was

silent for a moment. "Say, partner, there's some-thin' I been meanin' to tell you, but it sort of slipped my mind."

Willoughby groaned and pulled himself back from the faint haze of sleep. "What now?"

"Back in Seguin. That town was sure fillin' up with Clantons in a hurry. Counted three of 'em, all packin' more artillery than General Sherman hauled through Georgia. But I reckon they won't find us, now that we got us a patron saint and all." Brubs sighed. "All we got to watch out for is that Delgado and his bunch. Don't you fret it none, though. Get some sleep."

Willoughby's eyes popped open. "Brubs McCallan," he said grumpily, "you are a pure comfort to a man."

Dave Willoughby squirmed deeper into the washtub of steaming, soapy water and let the exhaustion drain from his muscles.

He had welcomed the sight of the small adobe shack north of LaQuesta as if it had been the swankiest hotel in Cincinnati. He was home.

Willoughby reached for the cloth beside the tub and started scrubbing more than a week of trail grime from his face and neck. Brubs squat-ted at the edge of the fireplace and counted the stack of American greenbacks and Mexican silver for the third time, humming "The Bonnie Blue Flag." Willoughby didn't mind the racket.

"Dave, son," Brubs said happily, "we got bet-ter than eight hundred dollars here. Why, we won't have to hit us a lick of work all winter, we don't want to. Ain't it a caution, how easy it is to make money in this here horse business?"

Willoughby squinted through the slathers of soap across his eyes. "I wouldn't say it was especially easy. In case it's slipped what mind you have left, we've been shot at, almost scalped by Indians, run over by wild horses, nearly drowned in flooded rivers, and barely escaped hanging at least twice. And that's just in the last year."

"Yeah, we have had us some fun, all right," Brubs said. "It's like with women. The chousin's near as much fun as the catchin'." He tucked the money inside an Arbuckle's coffee can, put it in the shallow hole under the fireplace keystone, and clapped the brick back in place.

Willoughby scrubbed at his hair until he finally coaxed a sizable wad of lather from the remnants of the soap.

Brubs said, "Never seen a man so dead set on washin' off good old Texas dirt." He sighed. "I reckon you're gonna expect me to do the same."

Willoughby lifted sudsy eyebrows. "It *is* September, Brubs. I think."

Brubs said, "See there, partner? You done quit worryin' what time it is or what month it is. You're getting sure 'nuff Texanized." He reached into a saddlebag beside the fireplace and brought out a pint bottle. "Been savin' this for a special occasion, amigo. I reckon this here's it. We got home with our hides all in one piece — and rich men to boot. Have a snort. It'll cut the dust from your gizzard."

Willoughby puffed a bit of lather from his lips and reached for the bottle. He downed a swig, winced, and sputtered, his eyes watering. "What the hell is that stuff?"

Brubs said, "Thought it might be good. Cost a whole quarter for just a pint." He tipped the bottle up, swallowed twice, and sighed. "Purest home corn squeezin's this side of the Tennessee hills," he said reverently. "Got to be a hundred-thirty proof. Want another?"

Willoughby shook his head. His gut was still ablaze from the one drink.

Brubs carried the pint bottle to the table, fetched a mug from the mantel shelf, and toed out a chair. "Yes, sir," he said, "we done had us a mighty fine drive this last time out. Didn't have no trouble at all."

Willoughby reached for the horsehair scrub brush. The soap and water gradually chased the exhaustion from his arms and legs. He had to admit Brubs was right. This last drive had gone well. The horses, trail-wise, herd-gentle — and most important, footsore and tired — had tried to stampede only once, when a bolt of lightning hit a piñon tree near their Big Bend camp during a monumental thunderstorm. They had run only a half mile or so before Dave and the big roan managed to turn the leaders. And Brubs had done better than expected, too. He had only gotten lost twice in the Sonoran Desert before finding Don Alejandro Gonzales de Cuellar's ranch headquarters. The Texas Horsetrading Company now had enough money to see the partners through the coming winter in comfort.

Willoughby stood, rinsing the soap from his body as best he could — and started at the pound of hoofbeats in the front yard. The hooves clattered to a stop, followed quickly by an urgent rapping on the cabin door. Before he could call out, Brubs strode to the door and swung it open.

Katherine Symms stood in the doorway, a worried look on her round face.

Brubs swung the door wide. "Come on in, Kat. Make yourself to home."

Willoughby snatched at a towel.

"Relax, partner," Brubs said. "Kat ain't gonna see nothin' she ain't played with before." He turned back to the blonde. "We was gonna come see you just as soon as old Dave here got hisself to smellin' good."

"That's not why I came, Brubs," Kat said solemnly. "Those men you asked me to watch out for. Four of them. They're here. Down at the saloon."

Brubs's eyes narrowed. "Wondered how long it'd take them boys to show up. Been expectin' them."

"Brubs," Willoughby almost squawked, "what do you mean, you've been expecting them?"

"They been followin' us four, five days," Brubs said casually.

Willoughby stepped out of the tub and reached

for his pants, his skin still wet. "Why the hell didn't you say something?"

"Didn't figure to fret you none till I knowed for sure, seein' as to how you get the vapors so easy," Brubs said "Thought we'd shook 'em down in the Sonoran Desert when you was givin' me what for, thinkin' I'd got lost. Reckon they're better trackers than I give 'em credit for."

Willoughby was almost fully dressed now. He reached for his pistol belt. "Who are they?"

"Clantons, most likely." Brubs reached for his rifle.

THIRTEEN

"Brubs, I don't like that look on your face. What are you going to do?"

The Texan snorted in disgust. "I done got me a bellyful of Clantons. Like old Stump said before he charged Delgado, by God, it stops here. One way or another. And I ain't gonna have 'em shootin' up my house."

"Wait up a minute. I'm going with you," Willoughby said.

"Dave, I know this ain't your kind of fight. You don't want to deal in, I won't hold it agin you."

Willoughby shook his head. "I can't let you face four men alone. We're partners, Brubs. That isn't something a man can just turn off, like blowing out a lamp."

"You sure about that?"

"I have," Willoughby said grimly, "never been seriouser." He buckled the pistol belt around his waist.

A hint of a smile touched Brubs's lips. "Better wipe that lather off your chin, then. I can't have you walkin' into no shoot-out with a soap goatee." He said to Kat, "We're mighty obliged that you come out here to warn us. It might be best you stayed here till this is done with." He nodded toward the chair at the table. "Have yourself a drink. We'll be back shortly."

"And if you aren't?"

"Then, honey," Brubs said, "you can drink that whole bottle, on account of we won't be needin' it none." He paused for a moment, his forehead wrinkled in thought, then propped his rifle against the door. He plucked a linen duster from a peg, slipped it on, and pulled the spare .45 Colt from the saddlebags. "This old gun's got a good record on Clantons so far. Might as well trust her one more time." He slipped the pistol into the right-hand pocket of the duster, picked up his rifle, then said to Willoughby "Grab Stump's old twelve-bore, partner. Smoothbore's better'n a pistol for close-in work." His grin looked a bit forced. "Besides, I seen you use a handgun. Maybe with a scattergun you can hit somethin'. I'll fetch the horses. I may be goin' to a gunfight, but I sure as hell ain't walkin' to it."

Willoughby dismounted behind an abandoned jacal thirty yards from the rear entrance of Symms's Dry Godds and Salon, Stump Hankins's old twelve-gauge double-barrel cradled in the crook of an elbow. He glanced at Brubs as he tied the black's reins to a rafter beam of the crumbling adobe hut.

"Brubs, isn't there a better way to do this? After all, there are four of them."

"No, by God," Brubs snapped. His normally ruddy face was dark with anger, jaw set and brow wrinkled. "I'm gettin' damn tired of Clantons.

We didn't start this, but we're gonna end it. Right here."

"We could just get the drop on them, take their guns and make them move on."

Brubs's eyes seemed to burn with an inner heat. "They'd just come back. And bring more of their kin with them, if they've got any left."

Willoughby cracked the action on the shotgun, checking for the third time that shells were chambered. "I guess you have a point. I'm with you. It's just that I've never seen you like this before . . ." His voice trailed away.

"This here is a war, and it's done got personal." Brubs pulled his old Henry from the rifle boot. "I'll wait till you get to the back door. Then I'll go in the front." He picked the slack from the reins of the gray mustang. "It's gonna be chancy in there, partner."

Willoughby forced a snort of mock contempt. "Since when has chancy made a difference to you, Brubs McCallan? At least this time I know what I'm walking into."

Brubs nodded. "Anytime you're ready."

Willoughby gritted his teeth and started a cautious stalk toward the back of the LaQuesta saloon, using whatever scant cover was available. The shotgun receiver was slick with sweat in his hand by the time he reached the wall beside the sagging rear door, which stood open to catch the breeze that waited through the shimmering heat waves of a blistering mid-afternoon sun,

He glanced toward the abandoned jacal. Brubs

was nowhere in sight. Willoughby thumbed the heavy hammers of the double smoothbore to full cock, pressed himself against the rough wall, and waited. He became aware of the heavy pounding of his heart against his ribs and the shallow quickness of his own breathing. The rumble of voices from inside was indistinct, muffled by the walls and the heavy, sultry heat. He twitched involuntarily when the front door banged shut.

Brubs was inside.

Willoughby crouched and slipped through the open door, his body braced against the possible impact of lead if he were noticed. The shock never came. Willoughby blinked rapidly to help his eyes adjust to the dim interior. The hazy shadows snapped into focus. Barley Symms lay facedown behind the bar, drunk or dead; Willoughby didn't stop to worry which.

Three men stood at the bar, a bottle sharing space with a Winchester on the counter before them. A fourth, taller and more slender than the others, lounged against a support beam several feet away. All four were staring toward the stocky figure just inside the front door. Brubs carried the Henry in his left hand, his right thrust into the pocket of the duster.

"I hear you boys been lookin' for me." His words were soft but clear in the sudden tense silence. "I reckon you found me."

The men at the bar edged a few feet apart. Willoughby glanced at the slender man at the support post. The man slowly put down his beer and let his right hand drop to the holstered pistol at his hip. Willoughby sensed the lanky man to be the most dangerous of the four. That man would take the first barrel. The ease with which he picked his target surprised Willoughby.

"Damn, Hake," Brubs said, "I was hopin' you wouldn't be with this bunch. I sort of took a likin' to you."

The big man with one eye nodded. "I had to come McCallan. Jake and Ed and Ely was family." Hake put his hand on the Winchester at the bar. The others gripped the butts of revolvers. "You killed three Clantons already. You won't kill any more."

"I doubt that, Hake," Brubs said calmly. "I count four in here. That'll make seven."

For a couple of heartbeats no one moved in the thick tension of the barroom. Then the big man's shoulder twitched, and light flashed on metal as he swept the rifle toward Brubs. Fire sprouted from the pocket of Brubs's duster. Hake's shoulders jerked as the muzzle blast of the pistol thundered in the small room; the impact of Brubs's .45 slug jolted Hake's aim off. The Winchester cracked, the slug slapping harmlessly into the wall behind Brubs.

The slender man at the support post whipped his revolver from the holster. Willoughby yanked the front trigger of the smoothbore. The shot charge slammed into the man's chest, picked him off his feet, and threw him backward.

The heavy cough of the shotgun caught the

remaining two men by surprise; one froze for a split second in indecision. It cost him. Brubs's hidden Colt blasted again. The gunman staggered back against the bar, his mouth open in shock; the pistol dropped from his hand and thumped onto the sawdust floor. The muzzle of the fourth man's Colt swung toward Brubs. Willoughby dropped to one knee, slapped the shotgun barrels toward the gunman, and yanked the trigger. The smoothbore blast came almost atop the crack of the pistol shot. Willoughby's buckshot load went low, knocked the man's legs from under him, and put him down.

Willoughby dropped the shotgun and grabbed at his holstered Colt. His heart sank as his sweat-slicked hand slipped on the pistol grips. Hake recovered his balance, racked a fresh round into the Winchester, and swung the muzzle up toward Brubs. Then the rifle spun away as a slug from Brubs's .45 took away the back of Hake's head.

Willoughby finally managed to yank his Colt free, thumbed the hammer back, and squinted through the thick cloud of black powder smoke. One of the downed men rose to a knee, a pistol in his hand.

"Watch it, Brubs!" Willoughby yanked the trigger as he yelled. His unaimed shot kicked splinters from the bar a good two feet away from the gunman. The Clanton man's pistol barked a split second before Brubs's slug ripped into his shoulder. The big man's body jerked. He struggled to recock the pistol. Willoughby lined the

237

sights and squeezed the trigger. The big man's breath left in a whoosh as the slug caught him high in the rib cage. The pistol tumbled from numbed fingers and dropped to the floor.

A sudden silence fell in Symms's saloon. Willoughby shook his head, trying to chase away the ringing in his ears from the concussion of big-bore weapons fired in a confined space. "Brubs, are you all right?" he called.

"Think so," came the nonchalant reply. "Ain't nothin' leakin' out. You?"

"I'm all right! Watch it! A couple of these men may not be dead yet."

A moment later Brubs's Henry cracked twice. "Reckon they are now, partner." He shook his head. "Damn shame about old Hake. I sort of liked the old one-eyed coot."

Willoughby rose, the Colt still in his hand, and whirled at a scuffling sound behind the bar — and almost shot Barley Symms. The saloon owner leaned against the bar, red-eyed, and stared in bewilderment around the room for a couple of minutes. Then he turned away. The retching sounds Symms made didn't help Dave Willoughby's own queasy stomach much.

The powder smoke gradually cleared. Willoughby stood, his knees weak and trembling, trying to ignore the smell of burned black powder, human blood, and death. He holstered the Colt and sagged against the bar.

Brubs strode to the bar, leaned over, and plucked a bottle from the shelf. "Reckon we earned a little pick-me-up, partner," he said. He twisted the cork from the quart bottle and downed a hefty swallow. "Right fair shootin' for a Yank artillery man. I reckon you're learnin'. Want a snort of Old Gutburner?"

Willoughby shook his head. "I don't think it would be a good idea to put liquor on top of raw terror while listening to Barley Symms upchuck all that sour whiskey he's been drinking." He glanced at his friend. "You might want to take care of a little problem right now, Brubs."

"What's that?"

Willoughby gestured at the pocket of Brubs's duster. "You're on fire."

Brubs squawked and slapped frantically at the smoldering cloth on the pocket of the garment. The last speck of red winked out. Brubs stuck a finger through the charred hole. "Dammit, that was my best duster."

Willoughby finally managed a weak grin. "Wondered what you were up to with that pistol in your pocket."

"McCallan's second law of gunfightin' survival, son," Brubs said. "Never walk in on a man without you've got an edge. He had to pull iron and I didn't, and that was the edge." He downed another swallow of whiskey. "Course, I had another edge, too. A partner with a smoothbore."

Willoughby's stomach was still churning, but at least Symms had quit retching. That helped some. Willoughby lifted an eyebrow at Brubs. "You said that was your second law of gunfight survival. What's the first law?"

Brubs said, "Don't get in one."

Willoughby said, "So what do we do now?"

"Nothin', amigo. It's all over. Won't be no more Clanton troubles. At least for a while."

"I mean with the bodies."

"Oh," Brubs said. He toed Hake's foot out of the way. "Well, we sure can't depend on old Barley to clean the trash out of this place. I bet he ain't even swept the floor since the ark landed. We could throw 'em over their saddles and turn the horses loose. But there's four mighty fine ponies out there. I sure hate to see a good horse go to waste." He took another hit from the jug. "We'll drag 'em off someplace. Bury 'em, if you got the notion to grab hold of a shovel handle."

Barley Symms finally pried himself up to bar level. He glared around the room, his face ash-white, then stared at Brubs. "Who's gonna pay for the damages?"

Brubs frowned at Symms. "That's our old friend Barley. Don't never inquire as to the state of his cash customers' health. Just worry about them silver cartwheels."

Symms grimaced. "Cash customers like you two I don't need. Every time you come in here you steal my whiskey. Now it ain't enough you just wreck my place. You got to shoot it all to pieces."

Brubs slid the bottle over to Symms. "Aw, hell, Barley. You're gettin' plumb grouchy in your old age. Have a drink on me. Looks like you could use it." He went through the dead men's pockets and came up with a handful of coins and bills. He counted out twenty dollars, tossed it onto the bar, and pocketed the rest. "That, and what you can get for their saddles, ought to cover the damage. We didn't make too many holes in your place. These boys stopped most of the slugs. You ought to at least be a touch grateful for that, you stingy old coot."

Symms downed a hefty shot of whiskey. "How about the six dollars these four drank up?"

Brubs leveled a stare at Barley Symms. "Don't push me, dammit." His tone was cold and hard. "I ain't in the mood right now." He turned to Willoughby. "Dave, let's get this trash cleaned up. We'll keep their guns. Might need 'em later on. I been thinkin' about somethin'."

Willoughby moaned aloud. "Now is not the time for you to be thinking, Brubs McCallan. Let me get used to still being alive first."

Brubs said, "Why, Dave, there wasn't never no doubt in my mind it'd all work out. Ain't we got the patron saint of horse thieves and a guardian angel both lookin' out for us? And I got this surefire plan to make us both richer'n a nine-foot stack of cow patties. It just flat can't miss. Tell you about it later."

"I don't want to hear it." Willoughby stared at the stocky Texan seated across the table. "Every time you get that glint in your eye, I know it's going to cost me some skin."

Brubs refilled Willoughby's water glass from the whiskey bottle purloined from Barley Symms's bar a couple of hours before. "Yes, sir, it's a right smart good idea. Don't know how come nobody's thought of it before. Surefire way to make a pile of money." He downed a swallow from his own glass. "Now, we done all right so far, but you know what our problem is, partner?"

Willoughby grunted in disgust. "Apart from the fact that we aren't the world's best mustangers and not exactly competent horse thieves, I haven't the foggiest idea."

"It's as plain as the nose on your face," Brubs said. "We ain't been thinkin' big enough. We been workin' our tails off for nickel and dime horse cavvies, amigo. We're gonna make us a horse drive. Trail a big remuda all the way to Kansas. Maybe even Nebraska, Montana."

Willoughby sputtered, "A *what?*"

"All that shootin' down in Symms must of plugged up your ears, partner. A horse drive, that's what I said."

"Brubs McCallan, you have taken complete leave of your senses," Willoughby sputtered. His words were beginning to slur and his cheeks felt numb. "I have never heard such a preposterous proposal in my entire life."

"It can't miss, Dave." Excitement sparkled in Brubs's eyes. "More money in one year than we could make in ten, way we're operatin' now."

Willoughby snorted in disgust. "Can't be done." He lifted the glass and downed a stiff shot of Barley Symms's best liquor, which was not much worse than everybody else's cheapest rotgut.

"Sure it can, partner, you just think on it a bit more," Brubs said. "We know for a prime fact that horses is bringin' ten, twenty dollars a head more in Kansas than in Texas. People in this country's gone slap-dab cow-crazy. Ever' rancher in the state's fixin' to trail a bunch of steers to railhead." He picked up his glass and leaned back in his chair. "But ain't nobody thought of trailin' horses north yet."

"Everybody else," Willoughby grumped, "has got a brain that hasn't been kicked out by some bronc or shot away by an outlaw, lawman, or Indian. That's how come nobody's thought of it." He hoisted his glass again. Brubs refilled it.

Brubs sipped at his whiskey and smacked his lips in satisfaction. "Why, over the winter I bet we could put together three, maybe four hundred good horses."

"Just like that."

Brubs said, "Yep. Nothin' to it, partner. We done got us a start — them four Clanton ponies out there in our pasture. There's ranches on both sides of the Rio Grande from Houston to Tucson to Mexico City that we ain't stole a single horse from yet. And if there's one thing I can't stand, it's a virgin." He drained his own glass and refilled it. "We can catch a few mustangin', too, should pickin's get a mite slim." He shook his head. "Sure would hate to have to stoop that low, though. Mustangin's damn hard work. But there's plenty wild horses out there."

"No."

Brubs said, "Dave, son, you are the mule-headedest man I ever seen, even if you are okay as a partner. What could be easier?"

"Easier than trailing three hundred or so head of half broke horses several hundred miles?" He downed another swallow of whiskey. "Through Indian country?"

"Aw, hell, Dave. There ain't that many wild Injuns left."

"It don't — dammit, now I've even started talking like you — it *doesn't* take many." Willoughby wondered why he was having trouble focusing his eyes. "And besides Indians, through country so thick with outlaws you can't stir them with a stick?"

Brubs let his chair down with a thump and leaned his elbows on the table. "Partner, we done proved we can handle outlaws. They ain't nothin' to fret over."

"I have earned the right to fret over whatever I want Brubs McCallan. And we ain't — we haven't — talked about crossing rivers meaner than the Rio Grande. Or prairie fires, or horse stampedes, or —"

Brubs raised a hand. "Dave, you're always lookin' for the storm clouds so hard you don't see no rainbows. Them things you mentioned ain't somethin' two real hoss wranglers couldn't handle."

Willoughby said, "Two men. Three hundred horses and a thousand miles of bad country. Nothing two riders can't handle, he says."

"That's what's botherin' you, partner?" Brubs said. "We could hire a couple youngsters to go up the trail with us. Lots of young Texas whippersnappers think they wanna be cowboys. Time they figure out it ain't such a glamorous life, like ridin' along admirin' their shadows, we'll done have 'em trained to the point they think they're havin' as much fun as we are."

Willoughby lifted his glass. "You have this all figured out, don't you?"

"Right down to the last horseshoe and nail, partner. Now study on this part of it — we could have us a mess of fun on a drive like that. There's some fine-lookin' women up in Kansas, Brother Dave." He paused for a swig of liquor and winced. "Better whiskey, too. Hell, I hear some of them Dodge City saloons even got high-dollar wine and higher-dollar whores."

Willoughby said, "Is that all you think about? Whiskey and women?"

"Nope. Sometimes I think about women and whiskey. There ain't nothin' else, is there?" Brubs sounded alarmed as if there might be.

"Stayin' — staying — alive might be one place to start."

Brubs stretched his arms over his head, flexed his shoulder muscles, and refilled Willoughby's whiskey glass. "Dave, I seem to recall once you said somethin' about maybe someday settlin' down, findin' yourself a nice girl, and breedin' up a passel of kids. Thing like that takes money, partner. Lots of it." He waited until Willoughby downed another swallow. "Figure on this, amigo. Four hundred horses times thirty forty dollars apiece. Say thirty-five, average. I ain't too swift at cipherin', but I reckon that'd come to nigh on to *fourteen thousand* dollars!"

Willoughby shook his head. "It ain't — isn't worth it."

"Another thing, partner. You know what that'd mean for business? Why, the whole country'd know about the Texas Horsetradin' Company three days after we hit railhead. We'd put LaQuesta smack-dab on the map. You think on it. I figure we got another three, four weeks before we have to start gatherin' up the first few head for our big remuda."

Willoughby wiped a hand across the beads of sweat that dotted his forehead. "You are serious about this, aren't you?"

Brubs's grin seemed to cover half his face. "Partner, I ain't never been seriouser. We wouldn't run into nothin' two real genuine Texans couldn't handle."

Willoughby moaned aloud. "God, I was afraid you'd say that." He lifted his glass. "No. I am not going — Wait a minute! What did you just say?"

"I said I ain't never been seriouser."

"After that. Something about real genuine Texans."

"Oh. Been meanin' to tell you about that, partner." Brubs reached across the table and clapped Willoughby on the shoulder. "I reckon you done got mostly cured of that Back East Yankee stuff. Why, you're ridin' like a Comanche, cussin' like a teamster, shootin' like a Ranger, drinkin' like a sailor, and whorin' all over the state. If that don't mean you're mostly Texan now, I don't know what is one."

"I'll be damned," Willoughby said caustically, "the red, white, and blue badge of honor with a star in the middle." He tossed back another swig.

"Dave," Brubs said with a wounded pout, "that ain't no honor to be took lightly. I ain't never bestowed it on no man before. Wouldn't now, except you'll do to ride the river with." The grin came back. "Mind you, I can't make you no real genuine Texan just yet, 'cause you still got some work to do. But back when old Sam Houston was gettin' ready to boot Santa Anna's backside, there was kind of an in-between Texas government. What's the word for it?"

"Pro—provisional."

"So that's you now, partner. You are a real, genuine, provisional Texan. Like gettin' promoted from private plumb to captain." He refilled Willoughby's glass.

Willoughby sighed heavily. "Provisional Texan or not, I shall try one more time to express my unwavering stand on this issue. No. The answer is engraved in stone, my crude and unwashed friend. I am not going. Not next year, not now, not ever. No. N-o, no. Not."

Brubs clapped Willoughby on the shoulder again. "I figured you'd start comin' around, you studied on it some." He glanced out the window. "Night's still young. What say we mosey down to old Barley's place and sort of launch this here new business venture by bustin' a bottle over her bow? And maybe see how Kat's feelin'? Bet she's feelin' mighty good, you feel in the right places."

Willoughby swayed slightly in his chair. "Brubs McCallan, you have finally managed the complete corruption of my sainted mother's youngest son." He rose unsteadily and reached for his hat. "In less than a full year, you've turned that innocent creature into a fugitive from the law, a common horse thief —"

"Now, Dave, there ain't nothin' common about us!"

"Who has on several occasions almost been hanged, drowned, shot at and even shot, was all but trampled by wild horses, dragged through thorns and cactus, scalped by Indians, barely escaped enraged fathers and husbands, dragged into a blood feud, engaged in a barroom gunfight with four heavily armed men, and turned into a gunfighter and killer."

"We have had us some high old times, at that." A worried frown suddenly creased Brubs's forehead. "Dave, you ain't been bored, have you?"

"No," Willoughby said thoughtfully, "one thing I ain't — haven't — been is bored." A slight smile tugged at the corners of his mouth.

He lifted a questioning eyebrow at Brubs. "A real, genuine provisional Texan?"

"One and the same, amigo. Dutifully conferred and swore at."

Willoughby clapped his hat on his head, slightly askew. "Swore at?"

"Swore in, I meant."

"Then let's go christen this new enterprise properly and, as you suggested, call on Kat. If I am to function properly as a real, genuine provisional Texan, I must not neglect my hard-learned habits."